Aftermath

Books by Sharon Ervin

Aftermath, 2008

Murder Aboard the Choctaw Gambler, 2008

The Ribbon Murders, 2006

Chick~Lit for Foxy Hens, 2006

Weekend Wife, 2005

Counterfeit Cowboy, 2005

Bodacious, 2002

Jusu and Mother Earth, 2000

Visit Sharon Ervin's website: www.sharonervin.com

Aftermath

Sharon Ervin

Deadly
Niche
Press

Denton Texas

Deady Niche Press
An imprint of AWOC.COM Publishing
P.O. Box 2819
Denton, TX 76202

Manufactured in the United States of America

ISBN: 978-0-937660-11-9

Dedicated to Bill
always my hero

Acknowledgments

I owe special thanks to:

- The FAA Flight Service Station staff in McAlester, Oklahoma, who once discussed transponders and speculated about futuristic tracking devices that have since become reality.
- Jane Bryant and Ronda Talley for friendship and being generous with their gifts for eagle-eye editing.
- Christopher Elliot, my research guru who has yet to be stumped.
- The firm but gentle critiquing of fellow writers at Romance Writers Ink, Tulsa, and McAlester's McSherry Writers, McAlester, Oklahoma.
- Publisher Dan Case for the validation of investing his time, talent and resources in me.

Chapter One

Wesley Stemmons opened the driver's side door, started to step out into the street, then hesitated. Was this the right thing to do? Was it time yet?

He didn't know if there would *be* a right time. Now was probably as good as any. He would have to bait her to get her inside, but it was for her own good. She needed something. This was something.

He pulled the door nearly closed, twisted and leaned his shoulder against the seat to face her. "Come on in. I'll fix us a cup of coffee and a pastry pop-up. Eating'll make you feel better."

Anna Fulenweider slouched deeper into the passenger seat and locked her hands in her lap. "I'll wait here, thanks."

Wesley looked out at loose sheets of a morning newspaper wafting on the chill October breeze. "Anna, I'm tired of you cowering around like some whipped dog. There's plenty of women who have ..."

The warning look she shot him stopped his words.

He returned her glare but couldn't help enjoying the look of her: the all-American girl, straw-colored hair; dark, almond-shaped doe's eyes; tiny freckles nearly hidden beneath the dusting of make-up; olive skin that bronzed in the sun.

He missed her easy laugh and the old arrogance that had been absent for six weeks now. But she would be herself again soon, if his plan worked. And it had to work. If not this plan, then the next. He would keep at it until he got her well. After all, it was his fault. No, no, he wasn't going to get bogged down again in all that guilt. Not now. Not when she was right here, close enough to touch, if she would only let him touch her, like he had before.

He studied her resolute face and his eyes narrowed. He could be as hard headed as she was. "You know you can be old-woman stubborn, for someone twenty-four years old."

Her glare, her posture, her snort of disgust, all shouted defiance. He needed to break her down, say or do whatever it took to get her inside his apartment. He was tired of seeing her like this, her high-edged spirit flickering.

"You don't want to be seen going into a black man's apartment, is that it?"

Her glower deepened.

"Come on, Anna, you don't know nobody in this neighborhood. Why're you so concerned about what someone you'll never see again will think? Are you ever gonna quit being uptight about salt and pepper hanging out together?"

Her jaws popped. "Stemmons, you're the racist here. Black or white, if you weren't the gutsiest photographer in the newsroom, I wouldn't give you the time of day. Why do you keep throwing the color thing in my face? Who cares?"

"You do."

"We're everywhere together."

The breeze whipped the driver's side door open and Wesley pulled it closed again at his back. "Because the paper's only got men photographers and ever since ..."

She shot him the warning look again.

"Well, these days you feel safer with me, is all." He barked a rueful laugh. "That's a first. A white woman less afraid of me than whitey because my skin's black."

She cleared her throat signaling, but he didn't allow the interruption. "Of course, the camera's the buffer. Tells everyone we're working. Keeps people from sniping at you. We don't want no one making cracks about what's the luscious white gal doing keeping company with the skinny black man."

Again she started to object, but he held his hand up in her face to stop her words. "Anna, I may just be an hourly-wage-type, uneducated guy, but I ain't unconscious. I see things. When I'm not carrying a camera, you hang back."

She straightened in the seat, jerked the handle and flung the passenger door so wide it almost pulled her out.

"Stemmons, I've been tiptoeing around a murder scene since before dawn. All I really want to do is go home and puke. You want me to purge here in the street, make people think your white girlfriend's bulimic?"

He threw his hands up aping a defensive posture. "No no, baby, not that. We sure don't want some stranger thinking mean thoughts about us." He paused. "When're you gonna get it? You're off the nightly news. You've lost your celebrity status. No one's looking anymore, Fulenweider. No one cares."

"No?" Her voice cut to a whisper. "Well, I do." She stepped out onto the curb and slammed the car door, before she strode around the back of the car and held up a hand to stop traffic while she jaywalked. "High profile enough for you?"

He locked the car and trotted to catch up. She might hate him—for a little while—but this meeting was necessary. Therapeutic. He'd goaded her, approached the forbidden to do it. He hoped the end justified the means.

She hesitated at the breezeway and Wesley stepped into the lead, guiding her around by the pool.

Autumn leaves floated, clustering in one corner of the discolored water. Plastic cups littered umbrella-topped tables. Tenants obviously still used the area, but October temperatures in Halston dipped into the thirties at night now. The swim season was over for all but the polar bears.

Wesley's ground floor, one-bedroom apartment was poolside. He unlocked the door and swung it open before he shouted, "Oh, no!" and began back-peddling.

The shout startled Anna who sidestepped as Wesley stumbled backward, yanking the door closed behind him.

"Come on, faintheart," a man's rich baritone taunted from inside the apartment. "You won't see nothing you ain't seen before."

Glowering, Anna stepped around Wesley and, displaying a little of her old bravado, pushed the door open wide.

Disgusted by her own constant, debilitating fears, Anna tromped forward, determined to confront whatever or whoever was intimidating her pal in his own place. Wesley lived alone. Who was inside?

Two paces into the room, she caught a glimpse of a bare white female bottom as it disappeared through a shadowy doorway.

A muscular white man with only a towel covering him waist to knees stood at the other end of the room grinning.

"Well, hello, sweet cheeks." He arched his brows. "Good. The boy brings fresh meat for the resident sheik. Take off your clothes. I'll get you a towel."

Anna withdrew two steps as the stranger started toward her. He mustn't touch her. Maybe he didn't know. How could he? But the nightmare wasn't going to begin again. Not here. Not now. Not ever.

She glanced behind her. The door yawned wide. Stemmons eased to one side, giving her a clear shot at escape. Wesley knew. He would help. If the towel-clad man advanced another step, she was gone.

Barefooted, the stranger was maybe six feet tall and sturdy, built like a lifter, and handsome, despite the annoying dimpled smirk. Hair matted on his chest and lining the center of his stomach intimidated her; marked him as being too male. Seeing so much of him—all of him, actually, except the part under the towel—offended her.

A tremor of revulsion rippled, pebbling the flesh up and down her arms. Anna turned her hostility to Wesley, the safer target.

Stemmons looked at the man in the towel and back at Anna, his face devoid of any expression. Then he began nodding. "You both deserve this, you know. This is fu ..." he looked at Anna and swallowed the adjective, "... ing ironic."

"Really." As the stranger took a step, sidling closer to Anna, she wheeled and bolted for the open door. But he was quicker, there in a heartbeat. One brawny arm shot out to slam the door shut before she could get to it, much less through it.

Blood rushed to her face. Her breath burned in her throat. She fisted her hands, fighting the panic. Trembling, she squeezed her eyes closed trying to dismiss the awful memories taking her back, back, putting her again inside the cage. Irrational, consuming fear smothered every logical thought.

Her trembling should have telegraphed a warning but Joe Marsh disregarded the signals. Beautiful women had instincts. They knew what they did to a man, especially one in his state of readiness. This was the kind of woman who put a guy through hoops just for fun of it sometimes, just because she knew she could. Still, he couldn't help noticing that she had suddenly gone pale and had the shakes.

"Easy, baby. Easy. Can't you see? You're this sheik's new favorite harem girl."

She looked paralyzed, except for the quivering, almost a vibration, which seemed to be getting worse. Her huge, dark eyes popped wide. He braced one hand against the door and leaned closer, thinking to quiet her as he put his mouth near her ear. He wanted to sample her scent, to soothe the peculiar frenzy, gentle her as he would any high-strung, fractious filly.

Anna's unreasoning fear burgeoned out of control. Her heart pounded. Cornered, she wanted to strike out at him and run, but her limbs refused to move. She choked back a keening whine and turned her face away from him.

Wesley barked a command. "Get away from her, Jughead. Can't you see what you're doing to her? Give her some space. Now!"

Anna's eyelids fluttered as Wesley's voice penetrated the hammering of her heart. Wesley was there. He would help; would rescue her from a leering devil again summoning the evil, that lurid wickedness, that lurked inside her.

The visitor's smile wavered and he withdrew two or three paces.

Cutting her eyes, Anna kept her face turned from him and dug deep for control. Strengths. Where were her strengths? Her advantages? Wesley was one. He was her friend. He knew her—her situation—had some idea of her desperation. She tried to get a handle on that stunning panic.

Also, she was neither confined nor bound this time. Squeezing her eyes closed, she took a deep breath and tried to think, to review the scene. The challenge. The man. She blinked and forced herself to risk a peek.

She felt tall, maybe even taller than he was. Of course, she was taller than most men. Also, she was wearing shoes and stretched to her full height, stiff and straight against the door, while he was barefooted and skulking. Although he didn't actually appear to move, his muscles rippled under his skin like a large feline. He reminded her of a cat toying with a cornered mouse.

As Anna sucked up her courage and ventured a full look at her adversary, she was surprised that he stared back at her, regarding her curiously. She thought again of the naked female who had bounded out of sight when she and Wesley arrived.

The scene was vulgar, yet the woman hadn't seemed frightened; didn't appear to need or want rescuing. She had scrambled only to hide herself from the intruders.

Anna's mind began to clear.

The naked woman obviously was there of her own free will. This man and woman were probably consenting adults. The situation was normal, both of them naked—or nearly so—preparing to satisfy their mutual need.

The paralyzing panic eased. Anna drew a long shuddering breath and prodded her mind to take up the reins and bring her runaway psyche under control.

She and Wesley had stumbled into a love nest. What time was it? She resisted the urge to look at her watch, not wanting to call attention to her hands and the infernal shaking which had not yet released its grip on her. She scanned the room for a clock but her gaze, instead, settled on Wesley.

Apprehension pinched his dark face giving him a twisted, comical look of concern. His eyes on Anna, Wesley moved closer and shoved the stranger's bare shoulder.

Wesley stood probably six-foot-three, but was pathetically thin, certainly no physical match for the visitor whose well-honed muscles bunched even while he stood at ease in front of them, oblivious to his scanty attire.

Wesley shouted at the abrasive visitor. "Jackass, don't you recognize her?"

The towel-clad man ignored Wesley's shove, which moved him not a step, looked vaguely interested and shook his head. "Come on, Lee, don't be selfish. We share the good stuff." Looking directly at Anna, he tried the playful grin again, dimpling. This time, however, his impudent air was less convincing. "From where I stand, this one looks choice."

Wesley glanced from the man to Anna and back before a sneer twisted his mouth. Nodding, he took a deep breath and said simply, "Anna Beth Fulenweider, meet Joe Marsh."

The stranger's grin withered to an astonished stare. His dark eyes rounded. His eyebrows arched and he retreated another step while Anna returned his stare in disbelief.

"You're kidding," they said, almost in unison.

Anna stammered, "Wesley, how did you? ... Why?" She focused her full attention on Marsh and felt a rush of giddy disbelief before joy flared in her soul and warmed her face. The last vestiges of trembling stilled.

Wesley looked a little smug as he looked from one astonished guest to the other. "I told you. The situation what we've got here is pure, ironic, poetic justice."

Chapter Two

Anna stared hard at Marsh, reevaluating. She owed him a lot. Too much. There was no way she could ever repay the man.

"You don't owe me, Fulenweider." Marsh said, as if reading her thoughts. At the same time he visibly revamped his demeanor, changing the bold effrontery to a respectful smile. "Don't be thinking that, Anna girl. I'm not anybody's hero. I was only doing a job."

Six weeks before, from five hundred miles away, this man had spent three sleep-deprived days and nights saving her life—not just her body, but the bits and pieces of what was left of her sanity.

She had recovered from the physical trauma quickly enough, but the mental anguish was harder to conquer.

She had been unwilling to subject herself to the offered therapy, bought and paid for by her employer newspaper. She chose instead to suppress the terrifying memories and her own ludicrous responses, refused to discuss the incident with friends or family or counselors. She had no intention of revealing those dark secrets or of reliving the ordeal, refused to expose what had occurred there to the judgment of others. No, Anna did not intend to talk about it to anyone. Not ever.

Tears blistered behind her eyelids. She didn't know if she could trust her voice, but she was determined to try. She wanted at least to thank him.

"If you think you're not anybody's hero, Marsh, you're lucky you weren't there when they found me." Her eyes burned but she resisted the urge to blink, afraid of releasing the gathering deluge.

Certainly, his body looked strong, but it was the man's indomitable spirit she had clung to during those fifty-three hours. She shouldn't be surprised he could read her mind here. Now. Hadn't he done that same thing throughout her nightmare?

Standing in front of her, he seemed to be doing it again, reading her thoughts, reestablishing their bond. She saw intimacy in his gaze even before he spoke.

"I knew you were in hell, sweetheart. Every second. All three days. Both nights, I ..." He stopped talking and eased a step closer to her.

She put a hand up, a palm in his face to stop him. He regarded her curiously. She wanted to give him more than a few kind words, but they were all she could muster.

"You were my lifeline, Marsh. A thread of hope I held on to with all my strength."

He spoke softly, "I know. I know, sweetheart. It was like I was right there with you. I never concentrated on anything—never felt so close to anyone—in my life."

He gave her a smile so slight that his dimples were only dents. "I was sucked dry by the time you turned up." He looked her up and down, a flirtatious glint back in his eyes. "I wanted to hold you that day, wrap my arms around you and let you know you were safe."

She smiled. "If I had gotten my hands on you that day, I might have hurt you, venting all that terror dammed up inside me."

His smile broadened. "I was beat but I probably could have handled anything you had left." He glanced down at his scant covering and flashed a teasing grin. "You can hug me now, if you want to."

She fingered the moisture seeping from the corners of her eyes, shot a quick look at the towel covering the only part of him that was concealed and gave him a watery smile. "Maybe another time. Thanks."

She wondered if the peculiar tether between them was something they could discuss. He seemed to have been aware of it too.

"I didn't know what that was exactly," she tried, "that link between us."

"Some kind of telepathy, I guess." He shrugged and looked at the floor. "I don't know. I guess we sort of wandered into the same mental frequency some way."

"Does that happen to you often?"

"No. You?"

She took a ragged breath. "No. All I knew was I'd found a secret source of strength. I sponged every drop I could get." Her uncertain smile wavered. "But I didn't understand it, especially when I felt your anger. What was that about? Why did you get mad?"

His dark eyebrows furrowed. "People kept telling me how smart you were, what a heads-up reporter. I couldn't figure out, if you were so damned smart, how'd you get yourself in a situation like that in the first place? I guessed you were snooping where you shouldn't have been. I got mad at you, for getting yourself into that situation."

"Being nosy is not how I got in trouble. It was a beauty pageant, for heaven's sake, not a crime scene. I was waiting for Wesley, minding my own business. I happened to notice something the pervert apparently didn't intend anyone to see."

Joe's eyes tracked from her head to her toes and back as he yielded a resigned sigh. "No, I knew it wasn't you. The guy's a wack-o." Marsh clenched his fists. When Anna glanced down at them, he opened his hands, but it looked like a conscious effort.

"I wanted to be here," he said. "They wouldn't let me come. The tracker's signal was weak. They didn't want me to break the connection we had long enough to travel. I asked a dozen times a day, believe me." His voice dropped. "The second day, when I could feel things getting worse, I begged 'em. I thought our telepathic connection would make me able to come straight to you if I could just get close.

"But after I guessed right on the monitor, they were afraid if I moved or changed the settings, we'd lose what we had. It was one of those atmospheric phenomenons; the weird way the beams were bouncing. The satellite signal was erratic. We were picking up a lot of noise. You know, static. The thing was a prototype. The one you had was an experimental model, like I'd told you. I had to keep fooling around with it to hold the signal. They were afraid no one else could do that, not even people who were several hundred miles closer."

He shifted his weight from one foot to the other. "It was frustrating as hell from my end, sweet thing, being that far away, feeling your fear."

She didn't want to get into this but she couldn't help being curious. "Doctor Ware tried to explain it to me, but I'm not sure he knew exactly how the telepathy thing worked either. Do you?"

"No. We just got tuned in to the same psychotic hotline, or something."

Her smile felt genuine. "I think you mean *psychic hotline.*"

"Yeah, well, whatever. Anyway, I didn't tell anyone about it at first. It was too weird. I finally asked Dean, the other guy who works there at the lab with me, but he wasn't getting any vibes. Nothing. He had no idea what I was talking about.

"That telepathic link was actually what got me thinking you might still have the tracker with you.

"It felt like we moved in slow motion. It took time to come up with a way to activate it by remote. I tried to stay linked to you mentally by replaying our phone interviews in my head. You sounded like you had a pretty fair grasp of the technology. We got to fooling around with the receiver, trying long shots, and got a hit. Being able to turn it on was a major break.

"Dean phoned the investigators on the ground down here when we got a lock on the signal. He also told them about the telepathy thing. They pooh-poohed it at first. Things got really dicey when I told them you were some place underground and about how you were starting to feel hopeless. Even the skeptics got encouraged thinking you might still be alive.

"At first, you know, I could feel the heat of your mad." He shot her a sheepish smile. She smiled back, nodding encouraging him to pursue that part of the account. "In fact, picking up on all that hostility, I thought the perp might be in some kind of danger from you early on."

He could tell the memories were bad. When her receptive look faltered, he again became serious. "I went ballistic when I felt you wearing down. Giving in. I could feel the fatigue and fear crawling through you like bugs."

"I kept thinking someone would come, but no one did." Her words stopped, but Joe didn't fill the gap. He just watched her.

"And?"

She squeezed her eyes closed, wrapped her arms tightly around herself and shook her head. "*He* came instead." Her voice was hushed. Neither Joe nor Wesley nor Anna moved. "Every time," she whispered. "And then it got so I was even more afraid ..." When neither of the other occupants of the room spoke, she finished the thought in a broken rasp. "Finally, it got so ... so I was even more terrified ... that he wouldn't."

Joe stared at her. "He left you by yourself? Did you tell the ...?"

Wesley shook his head slightly, mutely answering the question. Anna pretended not to notice.

"Yes, he left me."

"For long periods?"

"I don't know."

"Did you ...?"

She stiffened. Her eyes rounded and she began trembling again. "I don't talk about it, Marsh. I'm not letting that monster back in my head, with all his perversion. I don't talk about him or think about him or anything. I'm not going to. Not ever. Never again."

Marsh's voice was terse. "If he was that bad, I'd think you'd want to help the police catch the bastard and save other women or girls from the same fate, or worse."

A familiar hopelessness sapped her strength. She stood trembling and shaking her head.

Marsh adopted an indifferent monotone. "It was like I was there, Anna. I felt your terror. Sometimes it drove me right to the edge. I called Halston fifteen or twenty times a day, pushing dog-tired people who were already doing everything they could think to do. They had teams following up every tip, running all over the town and the campus and even out in the county. They assured me again and again: This was their turf. They knew every hiding place. They kept saying it was only a matter of time. Of course, time getting by was what scared me most.

"I thought feeling your fear was as bad as it could get. I kept remembering how bright you sounded when we'd talked on the phone. I liked your laugh and your sense of humor and your quick grasp of the work I was doing. I had a definite picture of you in my mind." He barked an abrupt, unexpected laugh. "You don't look anything like the delicate little bird I pictured. I didn't imagine you long and lean and built like ... well, like you're built."

She frowned and his smile dissolved to a silly grin as he eyed her up and down again. "I guess we can talk about how gorgeous you are some other time.

"Anyway, I tried to stay linked to you, to think what you might remember about the technology all the time I was ..."

A woman's bodiless voice rent the air from the hallway. "Jo-ey!"

Marsh's eyes remained on Anna's face but his expression changed from kindly to annoyed. "Wait a minute. Let me get rid of her."

"No," Anna said. "We shouldn't have busted in on you. We shouldn't be here at all." She looked toward the kitchen where Wesley was pouring steaming coffee into two small Styrofoam cups. She hadn't realized he'd left their little circle.

Her coworker glanced at her and smiled. "Come on, Fulenweider, help me carry this stuff."

She hurried to take the toaster pop-ups wrapped in paper towels from her partner's hand.

Marsh tightened the towel around his middle. "Stay." He caught at Anna's arm. She jerked out of his grasp. He gave her a searching look and lowered his voice. "We're gonna talk about this. You know that, don't you?" His eyes narrowed as he regarded her suspiciously. "You're gonna tell me the whole awful story, start to finish. I want to hear it. I deserve to hear it. From you. We can compare notes."

Anna juggled the pop-ups into her left hand as Wesley handed a cup of coffee into her right. "I told you, Marsh, I don't talk about it."

"You mean only to Dr. Ware?"

"Not to anyone. What's more, I'm not *going* to talk about it. Not ever." She shook her head as if shaking off a bad memory. "I'm not going to think about him ... it. It's past. Flushed out of my brain with all the other insignificant historical clutter."

"What do you do during therapy sessions then?"

Wesley intercepted the question. "They've scheduled her five or six times. The paper is paying for it. She won't go."

She felt like shouting to stop Wesley from discussing her personal, private business with this stranger. Her voice surprised her with its resolute calm. "I'm not going back there. Not to that awful place. Not to him. Not even in my memory. Surviving once was enough. The policeman who found me asked questions and I answered them. There's no reason to rehash it over and over. I'm not going to do it." She lowered her voice. "I'm not letting him back in my head. Why can't people understand that?" She glowered toward the floor with new resolve. "For sanity's sake, I can't do it."

Marsh's gaze was intense as he took a step toward her. Startled, she took a quick step back. He stopped but spoke, his voice resonate. "Sweet thing, I learned a long time ago, when you visit people after a catastrophe, a death, you need to ask what happened, and you need to let them tell it as many times as they will. The more they talk about it, the more they accept the reality of what's happened. After that, they can heal and move beyond it. It gives them closure. You need to get this out, expose it to the sunlight."

"Jo-ey," the shrill voice pealed once more from the hallway.

He grimaced again, his eyes playing over Anna's face. "One quick hug. For my sake, not yours."

He slid another step toward her. Again she retreated quickly, reaching back with the handful of pop-ups, crumbling them as she grappled for the doorknob behind her. When Marsh continued to advance, her startled surprise became terror. She shook her head. Her eyes, rounded with fear and pleading, stopped him. He shot a puzzled glance at Stemmons.

"She can't, Joe," Wesley said quietly. "See how it is?"

Anna put the wadded pop-ups and her coffee cup together in one hand, opened the door with the other and practically ran outside.

Stemmons groaned when the female in the hallway called again. "Get rid of that, Joe. Put on some clothes. Go with us. Anna needs you. That's why I called you. It's why you're here, isn't it? To help Anna? You're the one person who might be able to get through, who might help us get her back the way she used to be."

Marsh gave his friend a dubious look and attempted a smile. "I'd say she and I got off to kind of a rocky start."

"Yeah. But that's okay. I know her." Stemmons arched an eyebrow. "I know you, too, Casanova. She probably needed to set up some defense against the Marsh charm. This was probably a better beginning than you know."

Marsh shook his head, looking at the empty doorway. "I didn't realize she'd be so ... fragile." He paused. "She's not at all like I thought. I had this mental picture of some over confident, very savvy, petite piece of fluff."

"I tried to tell you. It's like you said a while ago. She's choice. And, I swear, when she's herself, she's feisty and ornery and more trouble, more fun than any female I've ever known."

Marsh flashed him a questioning look, but Stemmons ignored it.

"Sure, she may have had a few rough edges, but they was starting to wear down some. I just thank God we got her back alive. Her body came back pretty well intact but there was no way anyone could have known how bad she'd got tore up inside her head." He looked longingly toward the door. "The feistiness is gone, all that laughing and orneriness drained away. It's like he scared the fun out of her."

Marsh, too, looked toward the open door thoughtfully. "She's a fine looking woman, Lee."

"Tell me about it."

There was a moment of silence, each man occupied with his own thoughts. Finally, Marsh broke the quiet. "Those shakes, is that part of it?"

"Yeah. But that's not all. The cops used to have to warn her about busting into a crime scene with 'em. She was too gutsy for her own good. Now, she hangs back—way back—creeping around like a shadow."

Marsh squinted. "Will she let you touch her?"

"No. Won't let no one. Not yet. I talked to this friend of mine who's a psych grad. He said it could be a while. Maybe a long time. Maybe never."

Marsh resecured his towel. "The first thing I asked after they found her was if she'd been raped. I thought she had been sexually violated." He looked sheepish. "The vibes. You know."

Wesley nodded, but didn't speak, so Marsh continued. "If sexual assault's not the problem, then what's got her acting like this?"

"Nobody knows and she's not telling. Physically, she's okay, a little thinner but we can get that back."

"That's a nice body," Marsh said quietly.

"Yeah. But it's even better when her ego's working right. She used to cut me off at the knees with a word, me and everybody else laughing and loving it. Everybody'd be egging her on and she'd be grinning, watching, making sure she didn't cut too deep with it.

"That's the most important thing he took. Her spirit. It's the worst damage he done to her and I don't like it gone. I haven't seen her smile, I mean really smile, since it happened. No one's been able to break into that emotional crust she's got baked on over the tendermost part of her. That's what you gotta help us get back, man."

"Have you seen any cracks in that crust?"

"Yeah, but I want to see a whole lot more than that. I want her back like she was. I want to hear her laugh, make fun of things that scare her. That's how she was before. I want her back, Joe, all of her."

Chapter Three

"I didn't expect Joe Marsh to be so ..." Anna couldn't seem to find the right word as she sat with Wesley in the car still parked at the curb.

"Yeah, he's a good looking guy." Wesley polished off his pop-up and licked his fingers without looking at her.

She allowed him an impatient glance and took a sip of coffee before she halfway smiled and slumped back against the passenger seat. "You finally got it right, Stemmons—heavy on the creamer, not too much sugar. Thanks."

She offered him the other broken half of her pastry. He waved it off and looked out the driver's window, watching for Marsh. "Eat up, woman. It'll make you feel better."

She chuckled softly and the sound, so foreign after all this time, obviously surprised them both.

"No, it's you, Wes*lee*, making me feel better, dragging me out of one gory scene right into another."

"I wouldn't call the scene at my apartment *gory*."

A troubled expression took her face and she shook her head. "No, I guess not. But if we'd gotten there any later we might have caught them in the middle of ..." She hesitated.

"What? Anna, go ahead. You know the word. The *F* word. Say it. What would we have caught them in the middle of doing?"

She bit her lips, shook her head and refused to answer.

"There's nothing wrong with a little consensual fooling around, Anna. Sex. It's not an evil thing. Nothing compared to the murder scene we were at before daylight. Same way your own pitiful little experience doesn't compare to an honest-to-God sex crime."

Anna felt the demons inside come alive. "What are you talking about, Stemmons? To someone like me, being beaten to a pulp or dying would have been better than what happened."

"And just what did happen to you, Anna? Tell me. It's just us here, talking like we do. You can tell me anything and

I swear it'll never leave this car." He lowered his voice. "What did happen to you, exactly?"

She shivered, turned her head and cast her gaze out the passenger window. "I don't want to talk about it." She paused without shifting her stare. "I don't want to think about it. I wish he'd killed me."

"Hush, now, woman. Don't be talking like that. It's not like you, getting maudlin. You used to make fun of melodrama. Call it crap." He waited, but she didn't offer to explain, so he continued. "A lot of women have endured a lot worse, Anna, and walked away healthy, mentally and physically. You weren't even raped."

She pulled her knees up and wrapped her arms around them. "I'm not going to talk about it, Stemmons. I'm not going to think about anything but sunshine and light."

"What about when it rains?"

"I'll stay inside, leave all the lights on."

"How do you manage at night?"

"Like I said, I leave all the lights on."

"All the time?"

She touched her forehead to her knees but knew that, as closely as he was watching, he could see her chin quiver. Biting her lips, willing herself to straighten up, she held her position for several ticks, until she got her volatile emotions under control.

Putting her feet back on the floor, Anna dug one finger into the pop-up on the seat beside her. The filling oozed. Pondering, she picked up the pastry and bit into it.

Stemmons' expression and mood seemed to darken.

She breathed deeply through her nose trying not to gag before she said, "Can we please get out of here?"

He squared himself with the steering wheel and put the key in the ignition. Marsh appeared, coming from the breezeway at a lope.

"Here he comes."

She turned to look, a grudging concession, but wanting an overall take of this man whose mind and spirit had sustained hers during her ordeal—comforting, encouraging, challenging her, all by some kind of brain-to-brain communication. She thought she had only imagined it, but he was aware of it too, reinforcing her belief in their strange connection.

Marsh's gait appeared effortless. He wore khaki slacks, laced deck shoes and a sport shirt open at the neck under a blazer. In spite of his clothing, Anna could still visualize the muscular definition of his chest, the brawny arms and shoulders. He was an enigma to her, a man whose easy patter and dimpled smile were part of a disarming facade for depth he apparently preferred to keep secret.

Still, something about him intimidated her and since her abduction, she made it a point to avoid men who set off warning bells in her head. Consciously or not, she now shunned most males, but most particularly the sleek, predatory types. In spite of his self-effacing ways, Marsh triggered her inner warning system.

Startled by his answering gaze and his relentless approach, Anna looked toward Wesley. "Don't leave me alone with him, Stemmons. Please don't. And tell him not to touch me."

"You tell him, Anna. Whatever you do or don't want from him, it's up to you to tell him."

"But I don't know him."

"Oh yeah, you do. You two communicate just fine. How he treats you is your responsibility. Yours and his."

Joe flung the passenger door open, drawing glares from both Wesley and Anna.

"Move over." He nudged her shoulder.

Anna shuddered, twisted away from his hand, and leaned forward, her body language suggesting he push the seat forward. "Sit in the back."

"Not unless you sit back there with me."

Wesley snorted. "Oh, no. I'm not chauffeuring the two of you. I ain't no cabby."

Anna started to get out, trying to get around Joe without touching him, but he settled a hand on her shoulder. She tried to shrug it off without acknowledging the contact verbally.

"I'll sit in back," she said.

Joe grabbed her forearm near her wrist. She struggled to free it but he wouldn't release her. Instead, he stared at her, his face deadly serious. "I'm sitting next to you, sweet thing.

What's more, I am going to touch you. I'm going to touch you any damn time I want to. I've earned the right. Don't make it any harder on yourself than it has to be. That's how things are. Get used to it."

She opened her mouth but words wouldn't come. Tears glistened in her eyes and she began to spasm, her arm beneath his hand quaking as if it were palsied.

Marsh watched, let her struggle for several seconds to overcome it, then threw his hand up releasing her. She scrambled by him and bolted a dozen steps down the sidewalk, putting thirty or forty feet between them.

Marsh started to go after her but Wesley shouted him back. "Let her go, Joe. She needs a minute."

"How did she get like this? Was she this bad when they found her?"

Wesley gave him a hapless smile. "Worse. It was a lot worse before. That's the reason she only works with me. I let her be. I never lay a hand on her. If she stumbled, I wouldn't try to catch her. I know better. It's finally got so she touches me some. The first time, she wanted me to turn around for a shot and she pushed my elbow. It would have been nothing coming from anyone else, but I was flattered as hell. I figured that shove signaled some kind of progress. That happened three weeks ago.

"Since then, she's grabbed my arm a couple of times. Last Thursday, she caught my hand, flesh on flesh. As far as I know, it was the first time she'd voluntarily touched another person's skin since the abduction. You should have seen her. When she realized what she'd done, she got all teary and blubbered like a baby. I would have put my arms around her, but she wouldn't let me get within ten feet.

"Once she got through crying, she was pretty pleased with herself, like a kid who'd just rode her bike alone for the first time."

Marsh glanced toward her. "Lee, it's been more than a month."

"Six weeks, but I figure slow is better than no progress at all." He hesitated, also looking toward her. "It's my fault. I was meeting her at the pageant. I went to the auditorium instead of back to the dressing rooms. I was just sitting there waiting when he took her." He hesitated, then added,

"Snatched her out of the parking lot on her way into the place, they said."

"You can't blame yourself, man. What is, is what is. Why won't she do the counseling? Did she tell you that?"

"Same as she told you. She don't wanna think about it, much less spew it all out into the air in words. She takes pills to sleep. Just a while ago, she told me she leaves all the lights on in her apartment, all the time."

Marsh's eyes remained on Anna who stood with her fists on her hips, gazing skyward and taking deep breaths. A passerby noticed and looked up to see what she was looking at. Joe smiled ruefully. "Misdirection."

Several people—pedestrians, passing motorists—followed Anna's gaze. When she noticed, she coughed, cleared her throat and walked back to the car.

Marsh stepped aside to give her access to the front seat. After she was in, he waited, unmoving. With a pained expression and finally a groan, she slid over. Her knees were almost in her face with her feet on the hump. Marsh hopped in beside her and slammed the door.

"Put your legs over this way." He reached for her knees but before he could touch her, she did as he suggested.

They drove several blocks in silence before Marsh splayed his legs a little, pressing his thigh against hers. She shifted but moving away from him put her closer to Wesley. Marsh was forcing her to touch one or the other of them. Wesley seemed the lesser of the evils.

She looked at the photographer, who glanced down at her over his shoulder as he drove, and relinquished an apologetic little smile. She smiled back and relaxed, leaning into him carefully—anything to escape the interloper who seemed so bent on testing her.

She risked a quick look at Marsh. He gazed at the street in front of them, a satisfied smirk on his face. She was not touching him at all, but she was pressed tightly against Stemmons. She didn't suppose for a minute that the situation was unintentional.

But Marsh had not won. He might force her to have physical contact with someone, but it was, by gosh, not going to be him.

Marsh's leg moved until his thigh again was against hers.

"Would you quit?" She fixed him with an angry stare.

He didn't say anything. Instead, he withdrew the leg, allowing space between them, but stretched his arm along the seat behind her.

"Don't." She was getting edgy, could feel the uncontrollable fear simmering. He smelled of soap and starch. Oddly enough, those familiar scents calmed her. But, of course, he couldn't know that.

"I'm not touching you," he said.

She had squeezed as far from him as possible. "You're crowding me. I want you to back off."

His dark eyes were rimmed with black lashes. His expressive eyebrows, too, were dark, like his close-cropped hair. He looked serious, the playful aspect replaced by a studied sobriety.

"No."

"You have to help me."

He regarded her coolly. "You've had my help from the very beginning of this. And his, too." He indicated Wesley. "You know that. But you've got to punch your own way out of this. We'll help, but you're the star on this card. It's your fight, champ. Toughen up. We can be like your manager and trainer, in your corner, backing you, but you're the one that's got to climb into the ring and face the monster.

"The way I see it, honey, is you've set yourself up to take some punches, but you haven't thrown any."

She stared straight ahead at the traffic for a moment, then lowered her head and mumbled as if speaking to her hands clenched in her lap. "I threw everything I had last time out. I don't have any fight left."

Marsh's jaws flexed as his eyes narrowed. "Oh, yeah, you do. And you're damn well gonna use it. Yes, ma'am, you are, and I'm gonna stay right here, hang around real close, to make sure you do."

Chapter Four

"Wesley, I don't want to go to the paper," Anna said. "I'll work at home. Drop me at my place."

Wesley turned at the traffic light on Grand Boulevard and aimed his car toward St. Anthony Circle and Anna's condo.

Both men moved and started to get out at Anna's. She spoke without addressing either of them specifically. "I can make it inside by myself. Thanks for the ride. Nice meeting you, Marsh."

Standing on the curbing, Marsh arched an eyebrow, then looked back at Wesley. "I'm going to hang around here a while." When she started to object he raised his hand, palm forward. "You and I are going to talk and there's no way you're getting out of it."

She scowled at this man who'd guided her rescuers, prodded searchers, kicked ass long distance when she needed him. Again she reminded herself that Marsh's relentless efforts were credited with forcing the lunatic to release her. She might owe Joe Marsh her life. A lot of people thought so. Even said so. Now he was here to collect. He expected a lot. She exhaled, her resolve weakening. She owed him a lot.

She bit her lower lip to keep it from quivering and nodded. Her implied invitation was not exactly hospitable but, forced to it, she felt it necessary.

Witnessing the exchange between the other two, Wesley didn't turn off the car engine.

"Come on, Lee." Marsh started to follow Anna toward the English Tudor condo, but turned back as Wesley closed his door and shifted the car into gear.

The photographer looked up. "I figured you'd want to talk by yourselves."

"I think it'll go smoother and she'll be more comfortable if you're there. Have you got something pressing?"

"No." He looked away, then back at Marsh. "I mean I have some time. I need to get this film in the wash, but I can hang here an hour or so." He nodded, indicating Anna. "She's got a story to write and file, too."

"Give me that one hour, then I'll let you both get back to work."

Wesley smirked. "And you can go back to ...?"

Marsh shook his head and choked out a half laugh, half cough. "No, that was the waitress at the airport when I ate breakfast this morning. She was getting off work and gave me a lift to your place. She dropped me off. I thought she'd gone. You'd left the door unlocked for me. I went inside. You weren't home. I didn't lock the door. I grabbed a quick shower. When I got out, I heard someone. I checked the living room and kitchen. I'd just turned around to find her standing there when you came through the door. I was completely dumbstruck when I saw you had the doll with you." He nodded toward Anna who was halfway up the walk. "Then there we all were."

Stemmons turned off the car engine and flashed a satisfied little smile as he jumped out and joined Joe as they trailed Anna to her condo.

"Do you want more coffee?" Anna asked when they were inside. Instead of slipping out of her jacket, she hugged it more tightly around her, in spite of the warmth inside the apartment. Every light in the place—overhead fixtures and lamps—burned brightly. Both men looked around, obviously noticing, but neither of them mentioned it, for which Anna was grateful.

Wesley stepped forward. "I'll do it. Give me your cup." He took her small empty Styrofoam cup. "Where's the kitchen?"

Anna stared at him. "No, Wesley, I want you to stay with us."

Marsh said, "Okay, we'll all go in the kitchen then."

Wesley and Anna exchanged a look, both shrugged comically and nodded agreement. The interloper might be obnoxious but he certainly seemed to come up with simple solutions. Maybe he *could* help her. But she couldn't imagine how.

"So, how did you happen to think of the tracer?" Anna asked, motioning Marsh toward one of the two chair-back bar stools. She started to retrieve a chair from the dining table on the other side of the bar, but Marsh elbowed her aside. She didn't know if he was actually paying rapt attention to Wesley's efforts in the kitchen or if it was an act, pretending not to notice touching her, yet touching her at every opportunity.

And he did touch her, again and again, his elbow tapping her arm, his foot bumping hers, his gesturing hand brushing her hair.

She told herself to ignore the obnoxious man and concentrate on their conversation. Wesley was telling Marsh about the homicide they'd covered earlier. Only half listening, Anna thought it strange that, although she was brutally aware of Marsh's constant touching, it came so often and so harmlessly that her nervousness gradually ebbed. After all, she was in her own home, and Wesley was there, too, if there was trouble.

Apparently disregarding them both, rattling on about the crime scene, Wesley clattered around her tidy kitchen, loading the basket of her coffee maker and adding water to the tank before he flipped the switch to "on."

When he'd finished with both the account of their morning's assignment and coffee preparations, Wesley fell silent.

Marsh straddled a bar chair and looked at Anna. "Speak."

She knew what he wanted. "What made you think I might have the tracer with me?"

Marsh laughed as if the joke were on him. "It was a long shot but you'd just phoned that morning to double check the distance thing. Since every model you had access to would fit in a lady's handbag, I thought there was a chance you might be carrying it with you. If so, maybe I could *wring* some help out of our brief telephone acquaintance."

Wesley grimaced at Anna apologetically. "He does that all the time. *Wring? Telephone?* Puns. They're pretty corny but you'll get used to 'em."

Marsh ignored the aside. "Also, earlier, Scoop here," he indicated Wesley, "had sent me a copy of your piece on the transponder on that Cessna that went down west of Amarillo. He'd sent me clips to showcase his photographic genius. He said that crash was what made you curious about our little automobile anti-theft and tracking devices in the first place.

"The day you disappeared, I called Seymour on the off chance you hadn't had time to return the sample and to see which one he'd given you last. I figured if you had it with you ... eureka."

The coffee burbling was the only sound as its fragrance wafted into the room. Stemmons and Anna waited for Marsh to continue.

"I went for it. I didn't mention it to anyone because the idea was a reach, but I thought it was worth a try. Seymour gave me a list of the possible frequencies and Dean and I started fooling around, experimenting."

The coffee maker gave a noisy "whoosh" when it finished. Absently, Anna got three mugs from the cupboard, ignoring the used Styrofoam cups, and passed the fresh containers to Wesley, who sat in the bar chair closest to the pot.

"How do you take your coffee?" Anna asked, speaking to Marsh.

"Black."

Wesley poured. "Go on, Joe. What happened then?"

"Because you were sort of a mini celebrity," he shot a wry smile at Anna, "and because the police were short on leads, they were willing to follow this one, although I warned them it was shaky.

"It was hit-and-miss, but when we hit, that little device was the only one in town sending a signal."

Wesley slurped his coffee, a practice which usually irritated Anna, but which he insisted helped cool the beverage on its way into his mouth.

Anna kept her attention on Marsh who grimaced at her as Wesley slurped. She returned a slight, companionable smile, then quickly lowered her eyes.

Wesley shot her an accusing look. "Anna, when did you turn the tracker on?"

"I didn't."

"That's right. She didn't." Marsh arched his animated brows and dimpled with pride. "I did. Well, actually Seymour did, after I relayed instructions. I phoned the logic board designer in Japan. He speaks fluent English, which has been a real plus, and told me how we might be able to boot the thing by remote." He gave a rueful laugh. "Of course, before we ever started the tracking, or I'd even thought about the gizmo, I'd been experiencing these annoying little vibes. It was weird." He shot a warning look at Wesley. "Okay, weirder than my usual. I got sweaty, all emotional. Jumpy. I felt threatened. Pretty soon I realized that anxiety wasn't coming from inside me." He flashed Anna a significant glance. "It was you. Discovering that, of course, made me just a tad crazy.

"I started campaigning to come to Halston, to get closer, at least be in the same state. I told them I had to come to track the sensor, but my theory coupled with the tracker's weak signal, and these vibe things were all the investigators had. They wanted me to stay put, not get bogged down in the confusion of the search here, while they put my weird sensory perceptions to practical use."

He stood, indicating Anna, who had remained standing, should take his bar chair. She waved him back and perched instead on the backless kitchen stool. Joe eased back onto the chair and continued.

"By the time you'd been gone eighteen hours, I was a basket case. I wanted them to move. I could feel how upset you were and I was getting pretty damned frustrated myself."

Anna's eyes met his for one brief moment before she again felt forced to divert her gaze.

"At the twenty-four-hour mark," he continued, "when I could feel you splintering, I got downright profane. What was worse was that a couple of the searchers were skeptical about our link-up.

"Thirty hours in, I finally got a call that helped.

"Dr. Bergin Ware had taken charge of the ground troops. He said some pretty raw stuff to me, considering he was supposed to be one of the good guys. He and I had one very loud, very profane conversation before he got me calmed down.

"He said I was helping you most right where I was, inspiring the grunts on the ground here. He said no one else had the instinct or the telepathic hookup, that my picking up your vibes made me able to guide them better than anyone else could. He was the first to verify that what I was feeling was valid. I'm making our conversation sound a lot nicer than it was. Even while he was chewing my butt, he was boosting my confidence.

"By then people there were saying I needed some rest, but I was afraid if I let go, I'd never get back on frequency. You know, if I was rested and you weren't. Plus, by then I was feeling better satisfied that I might be doing some good."

Stemmons and Marsh both sipped their coffee but it was too hot for Anna. She preferred to wait until it cooled, another obvious sign, Wesley teased, of her minimal addiction to America's most popular morning beverage.

Marsh looked like a hero. Thinking of heroes in the nightmare, the image of Dr. Bergin Ware popped into her head, catching her by surprise. The meticulous, spare little gnome with his wire-rimmed spectacles hardly looked the part of a hero, yet he was the reason she was willing to tolerate the abrasive Joe Marsh now.

Sixtyish, Ware's booming voice was the only clue that the good doctor might be a warrior. The authority in his tone made up for the man's milksop appearance.

Ware had been the hardest for Anna to resist when he prodded and bullied and pleaded with her to open up. If she were going to trust any man, it would be Bergin Ware. She had not been the least bit inclined to confide in her parents who flew down from Spokane to provide moral support.

She glanced over to study Joe Marsh who was turning his cup round and round on the bar with one hand as he continued speaking, seemingly addressing his remarks to the coffee.

"In spite of my instincts, Ware insisted I stay where I was and that I continue to monitor you. Relay instructions. Meanwhile, he'd keep the people here focused."

Marsh's eyes met Anna's, catching her as she stared at him intently. He lowered his voice. "Now, sweet thing, it's your turn."

"Why didn't you come when it was over?" she asked. It sounded like criticism. Now where had that come from? And did the question sound as unappreciative to him as it did to her?

He swallowed a smile, obviously pleased that she had been aware of his absence. "Dean's wife was expecting their first baby. The little minx kept us on pins and needles two weeks longer before she finally showed up. Dean had to be off a couple of weeks after that. He didn't even take the full maternity leave the company allowed. But, I figured it had been too long by then, that you'd gotten back to your routine and forgotten about me. That was until Wesley called and invited me for a visit. He didn't tell me about ..." He gestured vaguely in her direction and shrugged, "you know, the shakes and all."

Stemmons cleared his throat, interrupting, maybe not wanting Marsh to say more.

In spite of Wesley's unspoken warning, Joe continued. "I can promise you one thing: if I'd been here when they found you ... if I hadn't had to wait this long to come ... well, I'd never have let you get in this condition. I guarantee. For sure, I'd never have let you *stay* in this condition." He flashed an accusing glance at Wesley, who puckered his mouth and rolled his shoulders, mutely denying any wrong doing. Marsh turned back to Anna.

"And I'm not going to let you wallow around in your misery much longer. Now, you tell me what you remember."

She avoided his prying stare.

Her reluctance must have been obvious, because he immediately tried a different tact. "Okay, we can start with some easy stuff. What do you remember right before they found you in the park?"

She shivered once and took a deep breath, resigning herself to the fact he was not going to give it up. She could tell him some of it, throw him a bone. "I woke up on a bench near the duck pond, in the middle of a clump of bushes." She'd dodged the bullet for the moment, but had a feeling she wasn't home free.

"Good. See, that wasn't so painful, was it?"

She didn't respond.

After a long pause during which none of the three seemed to breathe, he said, "Okay, now, I want you to tell me the one most significant thing that frightened you during the time you were ... gone. The one most important thing that made you afraid. Was it the way he looked? His size? His appearance? Something he said? Something he did? The single most important thing that got this fear working inside you."

She got up from the bar stool and walked to the living room. She could lock herself in her bedroom.

Catching up in a few quick steps, Marsh grabbed her arm, turned her and peered down into her face. Standing that close, he was much taller with shoes, but maybe not any more threatening than he had been wearing the towel.

She tugged to free her arm, but he held it firmly and lowered his voice. "No quibbling. You have to give me just this one thing. It's all I'm asking for now. What frightened you the most?"

She squirmed again. His eyes burned into hers and he lowered his voice to the coaxing tone. "Tell me that and I'll let you go."

She wriggled and pushed against him, suddenly aware that he was restraining her as he gripped her arm. She tried to yank free, but his fingers tightened. Almost against her will, her mind drifted back to the dank, humid, twilighted cage. She shuddered and shook her head, trying to block out the memory.

Marsh's voice was soft and compelling. "Tell me the one most frightening thing, Anna girl, and I'll turn you loose. I promise."

She heard the clock on the wall above the sink ticking; the coffee pot sighed. She was surrounded by the comfortable, familiar sounds and smells.

"My clothes," she whispered, and ducked her head.

Marsh tilted his face. She knew he was peering at her, trying to see into her head, to read her thoughts. Other than that slight movement, he remained absolutely still, obviously straining, wanting to hear her hushed words as she continued speaking.

"He took my clothes."

"All your clothes?"

Her voice was almost inaudible as she spoke to the floor. "Yes." She sighed. "All my clothes."

Chapter Five

Marsh released Anna's arm and held his place in front of her, motionless, staring as the color drained from her face.

Wheeling, he threw an accusing look at Wesley, who shook his head slightly, as if what she had said was news to him.

Marsh directed his gaze again at Anna who, although she did not allow her eyes to meet his, didn't retreat even one step from him.

He felt his own anger seething, bubbling through his limbs. He didn't like the mental image. He didn't like it at all, this lovely, intelligent woman stripped, degraded, humiliated. Although the revelation hit him like an unexpected fist to his gut, for her sake, he had to press on, milk all the information he could from the one disclosure.

"All your clothes," he reiterated.

She nodded.

"You were naked?"

She bit her lips, glaring at the floor, and nodded.

"The whole time?"

"Except ..."

"What?"

When her eyes shot to his, hers were full of unveiled hatred. Was she going to despise him for forcing her to talk about it, to recall her misery, or was this display of pent-up fury aimed at her abductor? Marsh wasn't sure, but he remained where he stood, not moving a muscle, waiting for whatever else she would say.

Wesley interrupted the heavy silence. "You were dressed when they found you."

Marsh flashed Wesley a slashing, murderous look. He didn't want anyone else to talk, didn't want anyone letting her off the hook. His gaze flew back to Anna.

She refused to meet it. Instead, she seemed to focus on the doorjamb behind him as she spoke. "I don't know when or how I got my clothes back. I have no memory of how I got to the park. I woke up wearing my underwear, stockings, shoes, skirt, blouse, everything, holding my purse. There was even a used tissue in my skirt pocket, everything exactly the same as when he took me. The tracking device was in my purse." She took a deep breath and shivered as a whine escaped her tight lips. "Then the worst thing of all happened. The rescue teams stopped searching." Sudden tears pooled in her eyes.

Marsh glanced at Wesley who looked as puzzled by her hopeless tone and sudden tears as he was.

Joe stepped between Wesley and Anna, blocking their view of each other. "Do you mean after they found you, that was when they stopped looking?"

She nodded glumly.

"Why did you expect them to keep looking after they found you?" Marsh stared at her trying to understand.

Wesley tapped a fingernail against his coffee mug, but remained where Joe had relegated him, blocked from her sight.

Anna studied her hands, locking and unlocking her fingers. "I begged them to keep searching. I wanted them to find the place. I wanted them to find him. But they wouldn't."

Wesley stepped around Joe and frowned into her face. "You didn't give them a description of the guy. You wouldn't tell them where you'd been. They didn't know who they were looking for or where he might be. How could they have found him?"

Although Stemmons had asked the question, her eyes flashed peevishly at Marsh, as if she expected him to make some other accusation. Finally, she murmured. "I couldn't give a description. I never saw him."

Marsh stared at her. "You never saw him? In nearly three days? What do you mean? Not at all?"

"Right."

"He didn't feed you or give you water?"

Her shoulders shifted abruptly and her body began its palsied shaking in earnest. She wobbled as she stumbled across the living room and grabbed at the doorjamb into her bedroom. Her fingers and knuckles turned white as she set a death grip on the molding on either side of the door, gasping for air, panting.

Wesley grabbed Marsh just as he moved to help. "Leave her alone, man."

"She's going to fall."

"Even if she does, you have to let it happen. Don't try to touch her when she's like this. You'll make it worse."

They both watched as she struggled and gradually regained control. With what looked like heroic determination, she straightened and proceeded through the doorway.

Perplexed, Marsh turned his questions back to Stemmons. "The report said she wasn't raped."

"That's right."

"Was she starved? Dehydrated?"

"No."

"He must have provided food and water then."

Wesley nodded. "The examining physician said she'd eaten and had had fluids. Her mom was there during the examination, to reassure her, but the doctor had to sedate Anna to complete the physical anyway. That's how bad she was."

"How could she not have seen him? Was she blindfolded? Drugged?"

"They don't think so. There was no sign of drugs in her blood or urine.

"I don't understand."

"Neither does anyone else. It might be hysterical amnesia. No one has been able to figure it out because she won't talk. The guy I know said all we can do is wait.

"Hell, Marsh, I don't care if she can identify the perp or not. I just want the old Anna back, the genuine article. Ordering me around, giving me hell."

Marsh regarded his friend thoughtfully. "Hey, buddy, get a grip. After what she's been through, that Anna may be gone for a while, maybe for good. I imagine if there's any chance for recovery, she's got to talk about it to someone, even if it's only you and me."

"Maybe so," Stemmons allowed grudgingly, "but this morning, getting out of the car at my place, she got a little fractious with me. I saw a spark of the old fire. And I was damn glad to see it. It could mean she'll rally without having to relive it."

"Damn glad? And you almost said the 'F' word this morning? When did you start cussing again, even the generic stuff? I thought you swore off that."

"I get frustrated just like anybody else. Sometimes it spills out, makes my language as colorful as me."

Marsh gave him a slow grin. "You're still spouting the same old line, I see. Still grousing about being born black. What are you now, thirty-one? Thirty-two? When are you going to accept the color of your skin and get on with living?"

"When it doesn't matter to anyone else."

"Doesn't seem to matter to Anna."

Wesley got what appeared to Marsh to be a ridiculously dreamy look and smiled. "Nah, sick or well, she's not much into color."

Marsh was suddenly suspicious. "What's this? The great black hope—the man who's always been immune to feminine wiles—smitten? You're not serious."

Wesley looked grim, shut his eyes and turned away. "Don't start with me, Joe," he muttered. "Really, I can't take it. It took every bit of willpower I had to keep my hands off her before. Now, there's no chance in hell of anyone, especially someone like me, making a move. She can't cope with normal contact. I can't let it show, especially now. Can't let all these tender feelings go running amuck. I'd give anything in this world if she could be my woman. She's all the women I ever liked best in one package. It isn't her fault the package is done up white."

"Come on, Lee, get serious." Marsh sobered, scrutinizing his friend, wondering at this strange development. "This ain't your first dance, son. I know you. You've had your share of ladies. More than your share. You've carried the standard for black men everywhere. A white woman? You're putting me on, right?"

"No." Wesley looked bewildered by his own admission. "I don't know how it happened, or why, or when, but that woman owns my soul and she don't even want it. I'm just a hair short of obsessed. And now that she's all needy and confused and vulnerable ... Well, that just makes it worse, that's all."

Marsh regarded Wesley thoughtfully. The man had been a black chauvinist all his life, at least as long as Marsh had known him, since they were four-year-olds in the same day care. They'd gone through school together.

The preoccupation with race seemed to have been born in Stemmons, rather than seeded later. How had this white woman, a blonde with freckles airbrushed over her nose, captured the heart of the stalwart black man?

Marsh knew one thing. He would have to tread this mine field carefully, tiptoeing so as not to set off Anna's recurring shakes or stomp on Wesley's tendermost feelings.

No wonder his friend had summoned him. He could see the tinderbox Wesley faced, trying to find a solution to their individual dilemmas—his and Anna's—at the same time trying to bridge the gaps between them. Wesley was wise to see he needed outside intervention. And he needed it from someone who knew him well, and who understood Anna's situation. Sure, he, Joe Marsh, was a natural for the job.

Except that he was feeling peculiar stirrings and a surprisingly personal affinity for this woman himself, combined with an eerie sense of proprietorship. Her condition, her need, her looks triggered more in him than casual interest. She and her predicament definitely required a delicate touch. He grimaced at his brain's play on words.

In running her background, Joe learned Anna was respected as a newsperson, and inspired confidences. Those who knew her commented on her humor, her instincts, her ability to reach into noisy rhetoric and extract truth. He had been attracted to her from five hundred miles away. Close up, in person, her allure was magnified.

Before, he had pictured her a small, clinging vine playing at being a newspaper reporter, biding her time until Prince Charming put in an appearance. He figured her to be like most females, willing to scrap her career for the life of a housewife; pictured herself lounging on the sofa watching soaps and eating bonbons, like some rich house-mouse types he knew.

He had studied the early investigative reports, including interviews with men she'd dated. Either these were the straightest arrows he'd ever heard of, or she was a genius at holding a man's attention without hopping into his bed. And she had discriminating taste. Most of them had been professional guys.

"*Anna's very upfront about her dating policy*," a female coworker told one investigator who documented it in Fulenweider's file. "*She doesn't go out with guys who've been married, no matter what their current status.*" Which, Joe had mused, eliminated more than half the male population over age twenty-five. "*Also, she doesn't date men she works with, convicted felons, or men over forty-five years old.*"

So far, reconnoitering, Joe was the only guy in her proximity who met Anna's qualifications. There was no mention of height, weight, or racial requirements in her criteria, but she worked with Wesley, which automatically eliminated him.

During the hours she was missing, investigators interviewed the successful suitors extensively and followed every lead on men she had turned down, those who did not meet her standards. Most of them were squeaky clean. None had priors, obvious motives, or the opportunity to have snatched her.

Marsh had poured over the collected information as it came in, during the dead time between telepathic sessions while he waited for the ground troops to track her. He'd put together a profile of his own, refusing to entertain one thought that she might come out of her ordeal dead.

Getting acquainted with her on paper had buoyed his morale. He daydreamed about the day they would meet, face-to-face, both of them alive. Back then, he hadn't let himself speculate about an alternative.

This had been that imagined day. Their meeting had been less than auspicious, not at all as he had choreographed it in his mental meanderings when she was missing. But then, she didn't look or behave as he'd expected her to look or behave. She hadn't thrown herself into his arms and covered his face with kisses of appreciation, as she had in his fantasies.

Of course then, he had not planned to be cavorting in a towel, accompanied by some horny waitress with flat, broad hips.

It seemed almost sacrilege to think about Anna in that context. Her long, trim, proportionate figure was round and luscious in all the appropriate places.

He chided himself, pulling his musings back to the present. He must not let himself think of her as a desirable woman. Wesley had first claim and the guy definitely had it bad. Over a white woman? Now there was a major surprise.

Yes, Joe would have to keep his hands off. Tough assignment, keeping his hands off while being hands-on.

This could get complicated.

Chapter Six

"Joe, I'm not helping anyone by hanging around here."

Marsh jumped, startled by the interruption and Lee's tone.

"I'm going down to the office and get this film in the fix. Tell Anna I'll call her after while about the cutline."

"What about her story?"

"She can do it here, send it from her machine. She'll be fine. As long as you're here, I won't have to worry about her." He gave Marsh a cursory look. "Will I?"

Joe shook his head, apparently a satisfactory response prompting Stemmons to continue. "After the early deadline, I'll break loose and we can get back to helping her. Okay?"

Marsh nodded slowly. "That's what I'm doing here, buddy. I came to help. You say stay, I stay. Won't she be upset about you leaving us alone?"

"Yeah, probably, but she'll get through it, if you behave yourself." He lifted a brow. "And you will behave yourself. We do understand each other about that, am I right?"

Marsh gave another solemn nod of assurance.

"And if she can survive you, it'll toughen her up a notch," Wesley added. "See?"

"'What doesn't kill me, makes me stronger?' That old *saw*? Yeah, I *see*."

Stemmons grimaced and shook his head, opened the front door soundlessly, and slipped out. Marsh poured himself a warm-up and wandered back to the living room to browse Anna's bookcase. Mostly fiction, some sports and how-to books. Wedding toasts. A wine bibbers guide. A couple of cookbooks.

Anna, wearing jeans and an oversized gray sweatshirt, her hair clipped into a haphazard ponytail, strolled into the room barefooted, frowning at pages in a spiral notebook. She glanced at him, squinted vaguely, as if she'd forgotten he was there, remembered, and turned her attention back to the notebook.

Her toenails were painted a muted mauve. He liked that. It showed some personal pride, was maybe an indication she was feeling better about herself, which meant maybe she was healing.

She paced into the kitchen and, judging by the sounds, filled an empty coffee mug. Where was her original cup? He peered over the bar to find her scowling vacantly at a cabinet, obviously trying to remember something. Marsh didn't speak, didn't want to break her train of thought or call attention to the fact that Stemmons was no longer present.

She strolled by him to a rolltop desk and slid the top up and open. The resident laptop computer looked odd, nested as it was in the clutter behind the ancient slatted covering.

"Can you call toes *digits*?" she asked. The question seemed to be addressed to the room at large.

How would he know? It sounded all right. "Yes."

She sat and immediately made the keyboard clatter to life. She breathed slowly, almost as if she had fallen into a trance.

Marsh settled back into the big, overstuffed chair which proved to be even more comfortable than it looked, propped his feet on the matching hassock, and switched on the table lamp at his elbow.

Everything in the cookbook—pictured in full color— looked great. He might put together a menu, get the groceries, cook something. Maybe even a whole meal.

He sipped his coffee.

Chicken enchiladas looked easy. And he could put together a spinach salad topped with feta cheese and a sweet vinaigrette dressing. His mouth watered. He flipped several pages. Butterscotch brownies. Yum. A little more complicated, but the recipe did not appear beyond his capabilities.

He poked around in the drawer of the side table, found a pencil, no writing paper, just a pad of new checks. He tore off a deposit slip and began jotting ingredients.

Really easy stuff.

He moseyed into the kitchen, careful not to attract Anna's attention, then decided he probably didn't need to worry. She seemed to be completely absorbed in hammering the keyboard.

He hesitated in front of the refrigerator and risked a look through the open bar, a straight shot across the eating area.

Sitting straight, concentrating, Anna was stately looking, tall, slim—regal, really—well put together with all the requisite parts, even abundantly endowed in places that mattered, at least places that mattered to him.

Her profile—her eyes focused on the screen—was awesome. He hadn't noticed the aristocratic nose before, like a Greek statue. Aphrodite, maybe.

He'd not even attempted to look closely at her earlier. He hadn't wanted to qualify as one of those jerk types staring at the cripple, in spite of the fact her injuries were not the visible kind. Damn straight. You sure couldn't tell there was anything wrong with her by looking.

He hummed to himself, allowing his eyes to move at a leisurely pace down the length of the woman, and up again, as the keys clattered. The guy who'd abducted her had taste. He'd give him that.

Joe frowned as a dark cloud blotted out the sunshine in his soul. What exactly had happened during those fifty-three hours she'd spent terrified and naked? It seemed to him like the perp had shown pretty near heroic restraint. Once she was stripped, it probably took major self control not to go with animal instinct. That part of this deal puzzled him more than anything else. That part of the guy's behavior was very mysterious. Very mysterious indeed. This wacko had to be even sicker than they thought.

But if he hadn't assaulted her sexually, what had put her in this shell?

And wasn't everyone taking a lot for granted?

The fact that her abductor hadn't raped her might not necessarily mean he hadn't molested her. Touched her inappropriately.

Glowering, Marsh set his jaw. Was that why she didn't want anyone touching her?

He arched his eyebrows. Maybe.

That at least gave him a theory to work, see where it took him.

He continued staring but his scrutiny didn't seem to bother her. Of course, she was probably used to men ogling. Any woman built like that, with a face like hers, probably got used to being looked at. As tall as she was, the guy must have been pretty strong to have carried her, especially if she were unconscious. Dead weight.

They'd been in the parking lot outside the auditorium with people everywhere. Why hadn't anyone seen them? How could the guy have carried an unconscious woman in any direction without attracting attention?

Police had canvassed the area near Lancelot Center and the field house, smack dab in the middle of the campus, a place alive with curious intellectual types. Yet they hadn't turned up a single witness.

Had she gone with him voluntarily? Was that the basis for her condition? Did she feel partially to blame for what happened?

He was damn sure going to find out. Yes, ma'am, sooner or later, he was going to know the whole sordid story, no matter how dirty it got.

He set his mind back on track. It seemed obvious to Marsh that Anna was imprisoned somewhere close. Of course, there were hundreds of garage and basement apartments, attics, walkups, boiler rooms, every kind of nook and cranny in the campus area.

In the initial police interview, before she'd clammed up, Anna had described her "cage" as "dark," She said the whole area "sounded empty," at least, that's the description that got into official reports, with no sounds of traffic or people, lawn mowers, nothing.

Did she know more than she was saying? Was she afraid to talk about it because she was afraid of reprisals? What exactly was keeping her silent?

Granted, if she hadn't seen the guy, she might not be able to describe him. She'd told the cop that the guy had whispered. She hadn't heard an accent. He made no grammatical errors she could recall. Margin notes someone had penciled in later indicated the man had smelled like yeast. Joe speculated. Maybe he worked in a bakery.

The cop who had taken her statement initially was only a patrolman. He'd gotten basic information, obviously figured she'd be quizzed by more seasoned investigators later. The important thing to the uniform was he'd found her. Alive was good, but murdered, she would have held everyone's attention longer.

Suddenly Anna glanced up from the laptop and looked directly at Marsh with unseeing eyes. He dropped his gaze. He'd been staring. Casually he opened the refrigerator door.

No wonder she was so slim. There was nothing to eat in there. A miniature jar of mustard, another of mayonnaise, a pint of sour cream with an expiration date from last January, and two bottles of water. Two carrots and a hairy tomato cowered in the hydrator drawer. It was a travesty to pay for electric current to keep this appliance running.

Well, he'd remedy that. He'd bring in groceries, tell her he wanted to cook supper for them here. He'd stock the fridge and pantry and use *his groceries* as an excuse to keep coming back.

He could hear himself saying, in all innocence, "I left ham and rye and Swiss cheese at your place. How about lunch?" A foot in the door was all he needed. He'd gentle her slow and easy, soothe the fractious filly into the winsome lady he was pretty sure lurked beneath the layer of doom and gloom.

But wait.

He needed to keep Wesley's interest in mind, be careful not to charm her, not let her get to liking good old Joe Marsh too much.

Joe stole a peek, peering over the ice box door. She was back on task. He couldn't help smiling, remembering her pithy articles he'd reviewed, all containing details that spiced her work and encouraged readers to follow a story to the jump page. He'd admired her well enough before. Seeing her had put a fine edge on his regard. He wouldn't mind if maybe she got to liking him a little.

She continued pounding the keyboard, seemingly oblivious to his being there at all.

Marsh finished his grocery list, checked the phone book for a grocery store nearby and settled back in the easy chair with a new Karp mystery he found on the side table.

"Where's Stemmons?" Her voice startled him, jarring Marsh awake. He'd fallen asleep, slack-jawed, probably snoring. He pulled himself up straighter in the chair, blinking sleep-swollen eyes in an effort to focus. She stood directly in front of him. She didn't seem alarmed that they were alone, only curious.

"He went downtown to develop the pictures." Marsh cleared his throat. "Said he'd call you about a cutline when he had them in the soup."

Joe fumbled with the book in his lap, losing his place. He took his feet off the hassock and shifted in the chair, pulling himself straighter again. It seemed disrespectful for him to be slouched like that, under the circumstances and all.

She frowned at him a long moment, then allowed a grudging smile. "What's on your list?"

"Um." He cleared his throat again, stalling until his mind sharpened to ready. "Groceries. I thought maybe you'd let me cook supper for us here tonight."

Her smile vanished, replaced again by the frown.

He shook his head. "I mean all of us—you, me, Stemmons."

"Oh." She nodded but still seemed uncertain, retaining the frown. "Okay."

"Lee took the car. I thought when you finished writing your story, I'd get you to run me to the grocery store."

She gave him a half smile. "I need a shower. How about if you take my car and do your shopping while I clean up?"

"That'd be good." He paused, studying her. "You don't know me very well. Aren't you afraid I might take off with your wheels and not come back?"

Her scathing smile returned and he braced for the cut he thought was coming.

"Actually, I was just wondering which would be worse: if you took my car and disappeared, or if you returned it, which means you'd come back. It might be worth losing a vehicle to get rid of you."

"Oh, that was low." He ignored her warning look. "Try to hold onto this concept, sweetheart. I am your hero." He thumbed his chest. "I'm the guy whose brain was tuned into yours in that little dungeon where you took your recent sabbatical. I'm telling you, sweet thing, I had it tougher in boy scout survival training than you did on your little adventure."

Her eyes snapped, flashing a warning, and her jaw tightened. "You don't know what you're talking about, Marsh."

His voice oozed disdain. "I was tuned in, honey. It was like listening to a ball game on the radio. Okay, so you got a little scare. Big deal. The stimulation probably washed accumulated corrosion out of your arteries. It's likely you'll be able to think clearly the next hundred years because of that little excursion."

She fisted her free hand on one hip, and looked exasperated before a slow smile tweaked the corners of her mouth. "What is this, amateur shock treatment? You are pathetically out of date and way out of line," she sneered as she added, "Dr. *Fraud*."

"You went to the center alone that afternoon, right?" he asked.

"Right. I *went* alone, but I was there among the hordes: contestants, chaperones, sponsors flitting in and out and in varying stages of flap all over the place." She raised her chin which gave her face a stubborn cast, defying him.

"I didn't know you actually made it inside."

"Well I did."

"And ...?"

She drew herself to her full height and took a deep breath. "I was sitting in one of the dressing rooms, waiting, listening, observing. I saw a hole just big enough to squeeze my pinkie into. A peephole, Marsh, for some little pervert—male, no doubt." She cocked an eyebrow. "It was at a suspicious level. I was curious. I stepped out in the hall to see what was on the other side of that wall."

Marsh waited and hoped she didn't notice she had him enthralled.

"There was a door. I opened it."

"And?" he managed, pleased that his voice sounded almost indifferent.

"It was a six-sided closet, dark except for light shining through all those little peepholes, all about crotch high. I imagine they all looked directly into dressing rooms. A lot of dressing rooms."

He tried to act disinterested, forcing his eyes to scan the room, avoiding her gaze, desperate for her to continue now that she had started, yet fearful that if they made eye contact, she would sense his excitement. "So? What'd you do?"

"I stooped to peep through one. Someone came into the closet with me. I started to turn around. There was a funny smell, vaguely familiar, a medicinal odor. He clamped a rag over my face. He had the other arm around my shoulders. He was very strong. I got woozy. I felt myself sinking. I tried to swim back up to the light and the air, but I couldn't. That's all I remember about the closet." She looked angry. "Now, are you satisfied?"

Marsh studied her a long moment. "The police report said you were abducted from the parking lot."

"The last thing I remember was being in the closet."

"Who else was around at the time? In the general vicinity?"

"No one. Everyone. Voices called back and forth. People were moving props and furniture, but I hadn't really seen anyone in particular, just a blur of activity. I was supposed to wait at the dressing rooms to interview some of the contestants when they finished rehearsing for their big finale. Wesley was supposed to be there somewhere doing the art for the piece. I guess I was early."

"Are you always?" He forced himself to look at his fingernails.

"What?"

"Early for interviews?"

"Usually. Punctuality's a big deal with me. It shows you respect people when you don't keep them waiting."

"Does that mean *you* do a lot of waiting around?"

"Yes, but I don't mind. I'd rather wait for them than have them wait for me. It gives me time to get my thoughts together, observe things, do a little snooping. Besides, when people think they've inconvenienced you, they're inclined to be more accommodating."

"Okay, so you smelled something medicinal. Then what?"

"Then nothing. That odor's the last thing I remember."

"Until?"

She shook her head slowly before her face twisted into a scowl. "I told you ..." As she hissed the words, her voice caught.

Marsh fought an urge to leap out of the chair and grab her, hold her, stop the infernal tremors that wrapped her in their awesome grip unexpectedly. The typed pages in her hand fluttered to the floor.

"Why can't you people understand?" She clasped her hands together, maybe to steady them. Her breathing became erratic. "I'm not going back there. Not again. The nightmare's over. I woke up. I need to keep those pictures out of my head. Can't you understand that?"

He strained with the effort to look and sound unimpressed. "Or what?"

She looked as if the insensitivity of his question produced an acrid taste. She swallowed hard and glowered at him, but the tremors seemed to subside. She didn't say anything for a long moment before she finally lowered her gaze. "Or maybe the next time I won't make it back at all." She swung her head from side to side, then stooped to gather the pages strewn at her feet.

Marsh pushed himself out of the easy chair and took a step toward her. She dropped the pages she had gathered, threw both hands up as if fending him off, and staggered backward.

"No, no, no!" Wesley shouted as he came through the unlocked door. "Don't touch her, Marsh. How many times do I gotta tell you, Jughead."

When she saw Stemmons, Anna seemed to shrivel and wilt like a helium balloon losing air.

Wesley hung back, wrapping one hand around the other which had tightened to a fist, obviously checking his natural inclination to catch her. She ended the maneuver sitting cross-legged on the floor, her shoulders slumped, her hands trembling, palsied again, at her sides.

In spite of Wesley's hissing threats, Marsh stepped over to hunker close in front of her. His voice took on an angry edge and came out sounding like a snarl. "Stop it. Stop it, now."

She didn't look up but whined and rocked her head from side to side. He took heart, however, as he saw the trembling diminish, and he pursued his new tact. "When you give in, he wins. Don't you see that? Just imagine that jerk, laughing and jiving, and enjoying every bit of this misery he's putting you through, even now. He probably imagines you doing this and gloats about it to himself, celebrating just as much or more maybe, than he did when you were with him. He feels it. I know he can feel you giving in to it.

"Damn it, Anna, it was only a tap, not even a body blow. And you don't have a glass jaw. Shake it off, baby. The referee's counting. Push yourself up off the canvas."

He watched but she didn't move. He put more volume and excitement into his voice. "Neither Wesley or I are throwing any towels in the ring, sugar. Now get back on your feet. Be a contender."

She raised her face and her expression surprised him, indignant, defiant, maybe mad enough to take a swing at him. He wished to God she would.

Pleased as he was to see all that hostility, he thought a little caution might be advisable. He tried to duck-walk backwards, a strategic retreat, but his heel hung on the carpet.

Flailing his arms like a windmill run wild, Marsh toppled and rolled onto his backside.

He heard her twittering before he got his legs untangled. She was looking at Wesley and appeared to be trembling again, but this time she was shaking with what looked like uncontrollable giggling. She swallowed but couldn't suppress the odd, gurgling eruption.

Watching her bloom with laughter, Wesley glanced at Joe then barked a loud, surprised guffaw of his own.

Anna sputtered, trying to say something but couldn't enunciate around her rupturing laugh. She seemed to get it nearly under control, only to lose it each time she looked at Marsh.

Joe meanwhile, playing it to the hilt, rocked on his backside again—more for effect than necessity, after he saw what his slapstick predicament inspired—and she exploded all over again, her infectious giggles effervescing, cleansing every vestige of morbid silence from the room.

Wesley roared boisterously, watching Anna from the corners of his eyes. Finally he eased his way around both of his companions, who were still languishing in the middle of the floor, and dropped into the vacated easy chair.

Marsh recovered a little composure, trying to interpret Anna's breathless attempts to speak. "Okay, Fulenweider," he managed finally, "put a sock in it. And try to remember, no matter how humbled I may appear on occasion, I *am* your hero."

His declaration inspired a fresh explosion, staccato nods, hands flapping helplessly, her sputtered retorts indicating he had spoken the very words she had been trying to say.

"You already thought of that." He winced.

Wesley choked on new billowing laughter, and Anna rolled onto her side where she curled herself around her knees, holding her sides, still victim to peals of loud, unladylike guffaws.

When her giggling finally subsided and Anna could again look at Marsh through bleary eyes without breaking into new hilarity, she lay very still. The room grew silent, like the hush after a storm.

"Okay, Marsh," she said, as she wriggled back to a sitting position. "You're right. You *were* my hero. Then." She brushed strands of the straw-colored hair out of her face, her ponytail in shambles. She tugged the clip loose and her golden hair tumbled around her shoulders. She looked to Marsh, like a mischievous angel as she said, "But what have you done for me lately?"

He stood, dusting his hands over his slacks, surprised by the veiled challenge. She was asking for something. What? What did she want from him? What would she accept?

She waved an arm his way. "Make yourself useful. Give us a hand up."

Obviously astonished, Wesley lunged but before he was out of the chair, Marsh towered over her, grinning, offering both of his thick, willing hands.

He was careful to wait, allow her to make the contact.

She slid her hands into his and all three people in the room held their breaths, each realizing the significance of the moment.

When she seemed comfortable, Joe pulled her smoothly to her feet. She stood in front of him, close enough that he could smell her fragrances. He had maybe five inches on her, he decided, evaluating their heights, but she was barefooted and he had on shoes.

Her eyes narrowed and she asked huskily, "Now what, coach?"

He could see compliance in her face. Okay. She was asking for it. Quickly he formulated a plan. "Square your shoulders, champ. Chest out. Suck in your gut. Stand at attention, like this." He stiffened and she aped his example. "Now, ball your right hand into a fist, like this." He raised his fist chest high and she did the same. "Now, do this."

He jutted his chin, cocked one eyebrow and twisted his mouth into a comical sneer, trying to look tough. Slowly then and with fervent malice, he raised his middle finger out of the fist, turned and shook that finger at the door.

Wesley chortled, gulping down another spurt of laughter, but didn't say a word.

Setting her jaw, cocking one eyebrow and sneering in an attempt to emulate the tough look, Anna narrowed her eyes, clenched her fist, stuck up her middle finger, pivoted, and shook the obscene gesture at the door.

As he collapsed back in the easy chair, Wesley hawked a coughing laugh which eventually mellowed to a sardonic smile. "I was right," he said so low that neither of his companions looked at him. "I definitely got the right man for this job."

Chapter Seven

The three-person shopping party returned from the grocery store sapped.

"How about we wait until tomorrow night to cook," Marsh said to nods from the others. "Let's run over to the Blue Note Tavern and Grill for drinks and food. My treat."

Anna scooped up the carton of eggs, the last item for the fridge. "No, you're here to help me, Marsh. I'll buy."

They wrangled back and forth without settling the question as Lee remained pointedly silent.

At the tavern, they toasted Wesley's wisdom in bringing Joe and Anna together; Joe's buffoonery for inspiring Anna's explosion of long-pent-up emotions; Anna for letting go, and finally congratulated themselves heartily for surviving the ancient rite of communal grocery shopping with their good humor still intact.

No one reduced to words their conspiratorial pleasure regarding the breakthrough in Anna's stilted mental state.

At the tavern, she limited her flinch to scarcely noticeable when Marsh covered her hand with his as she grabbed for the check.

He let her win, but felt triumphant that once again he had touched her without her lapsing into her wounded dove routine. He was relentlessly intent on epitomizing each tiny step forward.

Feeling warm and safe and a little tight from the ale and the heavy meal and clutching the tab tightly, Anna slumped back in the booth, allowing a silly grin.

Close beside her, Joe followed her lead, intentionally sliding closer so that his upper arm moved against hers. Tired of shifting all the time to get out of his way, she made a concerted effort to ignore his persistent touching as she listened to the clattering of plates, the clink of diners at other tables pouring ale from a pitchers into glasses, and the hum of voices throughout the restaurant, without attempting to eavesdrop on any specific conversation, which was her habit.

She felt comfortable and totally at ease for the first time in weeks, in spite of the pervading silence among them; consequently, she was more than a little irked when Marsh broke the peace and quiet with a question.

"Do you have any memory at all of how you got out of the performing arts center?"

She rolled her head against the back of the booth to face him and gave off a deep, warning sigh. Closing her eyes, shutting him out, she said, "No."

But he was like a bulldog gnawing a bone, hard to distract from his mission.

He pulled a small notebook and pen from his shirt pocket.

"Your last memory there was looking through the peephole from the closet into an adjoining dressing room?"

She felt a frown pinch the bridge of her nose as she peered at him through squinted eyes. He continued staring, waiting for her answer. She fairly spat it. "Yes, but I'm not talking about that any more. I don't care if you're offended, or not."

The man didn't even blink. "What do you remember next?"

She shrugged. "I've told you everything I remember."

"About the abduction?"

"Yes."

"How long before you woke up?"

"I don't know." The silence was awkward as he waited, watching her. Obviously she would have to say something. "It was dark. But it was always dark there. I have no idea how long I was out, so I honestly don't know."

"Was it nighttime?"

"I don't think so." She hesitated again. Was this man always so relentless? Yet, it was that same irksome determination that probably saved her life. Stubborn could be a good trait, she supposed.

She took another deep breath before she said, "I could hear machines droning somewhere off in the distance. I don't know how far away they were, so I don't know how loud they hummed."

Lord she hated having to regurgitate this, to think about it again, relive it. "I screamed."

The palsied trembling began with the recollections. She tried to ignore it, suppress it. Joe Marsh's body English indicated he was alert and obviously making an effort not to wrap his arms around her. He seemed to exercise firm self discipline as he sat, waiting while Anna bit her lips, clamped her eyes tightly, and pictured her mother standing by the newell post at the bottom of the stairs in the Fulenweider's family residence. Gradually, the tremor lessened and subsided.

"What picture did you put in your mind just then?" Joe asked.

Her eyes popped open. "My mom's face. I have to do that when ... It helps."

"What else helps?"

"Focusing on something non threatening. The newell post at the bottom of the stairs at Mom and Dad's.

"Why?"

"I don't know. It's solid. Trustworthy."

"Why is that?"

"Because it's wood, I guess. It's big and round and our hands running over it all the time keep it polished to a high sheen."

Joe thought a long moment. "Was there something metal in the place where you woke up? The place you were confined?"

"I don't want to talk about that."

Marsh wrote in the notebook and stuffed it and the pen in his shirt pocket before turning his full attention on her again.

He was damned persistent, and she was getting tired of his hammering at her.

Oh, she trusted him, she supposed; trusted that he was trying to help her anyway, not that she had any confidence he had a clue as to how to go about doing it.

Marsh clenched his jaws tightly to keep himself from talking. He'd almost decided she wasn't going to answer his last question, when she exhaled noisily.

"I woke up lying on a mattress in a cage."

He didn't breathe as he waited, didn't so much as glance at Wesley, although he wanted to caution the other man not to interrupt. The warning wasn't necessary. Wesley had gotten the message from Marsh earlier ... several times.

Anna's voice had little inflection. "It wasn't a bed. It was only a mattress, on a concrete floor."

No one else spoke. Marsh filtered out all other sounds in the crowded room, his ears tuned only to her—Anna's breathing, Anna's voice, what little inflection there was as she continued.

"There wasn't much light. The air stirred very little and there was always the humming noise." She bit her lips, as if holding back words. "White noise. It was constant." Joe and Wesley waited. "Sometimes the humming was my friend. It calmed me down. Other times, it was annoying, relentless...like you." Her eyes engaged Joe's. "It never stopped. It was like...a water torture."

Bitter laughter splintered from her throat as she ducked her head, glowering at her hands folded in her lap. Neither Marsh nor Stemmons reacted.

"It was cool. Someone had thrown a quilt over me. The quilt was cotton. Hand-pieced. Hand-stitched." She shot Marsh a quick look. "It smelled like fresh air, like it had been dried outside on a clothesline.

"There was a fitted sheet over the mattress. It was crinkled where it had been folded, like it was brand new. I don't think it had ever been washed. Underneath, the mattress itself was musty. It didn't smell bad, just old and stale, like mildew."

She thumped the heels of her clasped hands against the edge of the table and kept her eyes locked on them. Joe waited, watching, noting her body language. So far she hadn't recounted any ugly memories, yet she was growing noticeably more agitated. She seemed to glean strength from her companions' silence. The ale may have helped, too.

He risked a question to prod her. "So you were fairly comfortable there? Is that right?"

She shook her head, wrung her hands, started to say something and hesitated. She obviously was grappling with a memory, choking back words which seemed determined to erupt in spite of her resolve. When they emerged, however, they ran together in a rasping stream.

"It was dark. I was disoriented. I didn't know where I was or what time of day. There was light but it was a long way off, down a corridor from me, but where I was, was shadowy, sort of eerie. I seemed to be alone, in a cage, outside it was surrounded by cement walls." She paused again.

Wesley refilled her glass with beer from the pitcher.

Marsh ignored Stemmons and the movements of servers and other diners around them. "Are you normally afraid of the dark?"

She glowered up from under thunderous brows. "Don't be ridiculous."

Her companions allowed another span of silence before she continued. "There was enough light to see I was in a cage. A tall chain-link fence which went up and up. Chain-link also covered the top, like the aviary at the zoo. It was anchored at the top and bottom to metal frames which extended far beyond the room.

"It was chilly and I...I was..." She shook her head, but he knew what she wasn't saying. She was naked.

"I wrapped the quilt around me for warmth and got up. I stepped off the length and breadth of the cage. It was four paces the long way and three paces from side to side." She looked hard at Marsh. "As close as I can tell, the cage was ten- or twelve-feet long and eight- or nine-feet wide."

Marsh nodded but made no attempt to speak.

"I examined the chain-link, shook it every couple of feet, looking for a weak spot, one I could attack and break; a place where it would let me out. But it was solid. I searched every inch of the area, ran my fingers over the floor along the edges, in the shadows where I couldn't see. It was secure and I had nothing... nothing to use to pry at the chain link or cut it."

"Do you folks need another pitcher?"

Marsh jumped at the waiter's voice beside him, rudely returned from the scene Anna's words had sketched so clearly in his imagination. He had been mentally listing questions he wanted to pursue when her recollection stopped. He needed more time. "Yeah. Bring us another one."

Wesley held up a hand as if waving off any more beer, but dropped it when Marsh glared and shook his head slightly.

Anna seemed not to notice the exchange and handed their ticket to the waiter so he could add the new pitcher to their tab.

"Go on." Marsh prompted, not wanting her to stop talking now that she had finally begun to open up.

She grimaced. "Shouldn't we think about...?"

"No." Joe's tone was decisive. "What could you see from there? Describe your view in every direction."

She gave Stemmons a look, obviously appealing to him to intervene, but he looked away and wouldn't return his eyes to meet her glance. She took a new breath and turned to confront Marsh once again.

"I couldn't see much beyond the fence, in any direction. Cement walls. Gray, same as the floor and ceiling, stretching out in every direction, forever." Her eyes narrowed. "I wasn't afraid of the dark, but the starkness of the place did frighten me.

"Also, I felt terribly disoriented. I had no idea where I was or why or what time it was. I couldn't imagine why anyone had put me in that place, what I had done that someone wanted to lock me up."

She hesitated and gazed thoughtfully at her hands clasped together and resting on the edge of the table. "I tried to think who I might have offended, of someone who might have a grudge against me for something I'd written, some secret I might know or something they thought I'd divulge, but I couldn't think of anyone or any information."

Quietly, Joe said, "Who were *they*? Had you seen or heard anyone, at that time?"

Her eyes shot back to his, as if she appreciated the astute question.

"No and I thought that was a good sign. If they had let me see them, I knew there'd be less chance of my getting out alive. If I was not able to identify them, they wouldn't risk as much if they let me go."

"But you thought there were several of them?"

"Then? Yes, I did. But not later."

"Why?"

"Because only the one ever came. A man." She began fidgeting.

Marsh wanted to keep her calm. Obviously while her memories of the cage itself made her uneasy, they did not seem to alarm her. The fidgeting began this time only after she began to remember her captor.

Marsh concentrated on keeping his facial expression relaxed, while allowing some of his genuine concern to show in his tone of voice. "Being confined—the cage itself, even the somber surroundings—didn't frighten you, did they, Anna? It was the man, wasn't it?"

The meaty side of her clasped hands began bumping the edge of the table, slowly at first, then accelerating, pounding faster and harder. And her breathing quickened. She shook her head and cleared her throat. Her face twisted into a troubled scowl. Something important was coming. She was close to erupting with it. He could feel it.

She suddenly peered into his face, appealing for...what? Understanding? Sympathy? She had it. He was determined to give her whatever she needed, no matter what it was.

Her words came in a whisper. "The awful thing was, see..." Her next words were barely audible. "I didn't have on any clothes." Shivering, she inhaled. "Only the quilt. And I was afraid he was the one who had...you know...taken them...seen me...with nothing...."

It took all the self discipline Marsh possessed to contain the fury that suddenly came to a rolling boil inside him. The rage flared so quickly, so unexpectedly that he hadn't set up any interior defenses against it.

She had told him earlier that the perp had taken her clothes. He had known she was naked—had been duly indignant—then stored the information in his head. He had intentionally pushed it out of his mind to avoid this burgeoning, unreasoning, consuming fury.

Yet here it was back, washing him with the same tumultuous flood, ambushing his emotions, igniting the insidious outrage all over again. This time it was bigger, even more disabling than it had been before.

He couldn't look at her.

She was so lovely, such a bright, gentle, composed, dignified woman. He did not want to think how degraded she had felt, exposed. Humiliated. If he'd been there... Oh, he liked thinking about that, of being present, perhaps appearing suddenly, there in that place. He'd have taken such pleasure in ripping the guy's head off with his bare hands. In his mental meanderings, he dreamed the guy resisted, and he inflicted punishment to fit the insult as she watched, vindicated.

Of course, that was only wishful thinking. Hate percolated through his veins. Marsh rarely indulged in violent wishes, yet he longed to confront the monster who had left her scarred like this. He despised the man with every fiber of his being. Hated him for having looked at her, for having touched any part of what he considered her pristine body.

Joe struggled for a moment, breathing slowly, trying to bring his raging hostility under control, to contain the raw fury which might lash out and strike down the innocent along with the guilty. He didn't want to add to her misery. She wouldn't benefit from a display of anger or a tantrum. He was here to help her vent her anger, her suppressed feelings of helplessness, but he was certainly getting a clear understanding of how impotent she felt.

He reined in his rage with new determination. He needed to figure out a way to help her purge, to detonate a charge against her own inner helplessness, then clear away the debris debilitating her.

Unable to harness his indignation completely, he postponed it by promising himself his showdown would come. Sooner or later the culprit would pay for his perversity, for every bit of indecency that Marsh heard about or even imagined.

Featuring himself as her avenging angel, Joe gradually grew calm. At the moment, he must steel his emotions, endure the account, in case it got worse. He was pretty sure they hadn't gotten to the worst part of it yet.

Maybe she was right. Maybe it would be best for everyone if she kept all this poison to herself.

Wrong!

Sucking up his wrath and bringing it to heel, Marsh finally felt calm enough to look at Anna. Crocodile tears trickled down her face.

Wesley shifted, pivoting away from her, obviously too miserable himself to attempt to comfort her. Joe shot him a warning frown. She had held the toxic crap inside long enough, too long. It seemed to have metastasized like a spiritual tumor into a sort of metaphysical gangrene, putrefying her soul.

An ale house late in the evening was the ideal setting and he and Wesley appropriate companions. A lot of people got weepy after a hard week and a couple of beers, men and women alike.

Anna grabbed a paper napkin, wiped her eyes, and blew her nose. She shuddered and hiccupped irregular sobs. Both Wesley and Joe held their silence, concentrating on the glasses of beer in front of them.

Anna glanced at Wesley first, her eyes searching his face. Joe's gaze followed hers. There was no condemnation in Wesley's expression, only deep, deep sorrow which Joe thought might be some comfort to her, to see her friend feeling her hurt so deeply.

When she finally looked at Marsh, he gave her a slight smile of encouragement and a little nod, prodding her. "What did you say the dimensions of this cage were?"

Her shoulders rose and fell with a deep, uneven breath and she blew her nose again before attempting to speak. "Don't you have any empathy? Any sensitivity at all?"

"Yes. Where you're concerned, it's getting damn hard to take. Let's get this behind us."

She shuddered and waited several ticks of the clock before relenting. "Maybe nine-by-twelve." She seemed to draw some satisfaction from returning to the cold facts. "I finally figured out that the light was coming from an overhead grill of some kind several yards away. I saw large pipes overhead, above the chain-link ceiling, which was maybe 12- or 15-feet over my head. The chain-link walls were secured to posts. I tried to rip the fencing loose...kicked it with my bare heels." She drew her fingers up like claws and regarded them peculiarly. "I wrapped the quilt around me and I tried to climb..."

Tears streaming from her eyes interrupted her recital and Marsh looked closely at her hands. Cuts and scrapes had nearly healed but the angry red marks had not yet disappeared. Her fingernails were short, trimmed and filed to varying lengths.

Wesley reached across the table, an obvious effort to steady her, but Joe intercepted the offered hand and pushed it away.

She didn't seem to notice as she sputtered. "There was this pole..."

"Inside the cage?" Joe asked.

She nodded, again looking down, apparently to avoid his gaze.

"Like a flagpole?"

Another nod.

"How was it secured? Was it bolted to the floor?"

"Yes." She hissed the word and raised her eyes, pleading with him. Pleading for what? Again he found himself perplexed but determined to help.

"The pole frightened you?"

She looked startled. "Well, ye-ah. What do you think?"

He was baffled. "Why?"

"Don't you see? It's where the handcuffs..." She caught her wrists, one at a time, rubbing each with the opposing hand.

Handcuffs? Joe again battled to overcome his own reaction, forcing himself to concentrate, giving her a calming nod. He wanted to quiet her, but first he had to still the fury churning to life again inside him, firing the blood coursing faster and faster through his veins. "I see."

It took him several moments to get his demeanor under control and he hoped she would believe the delay was caused by his thinking, framing the next question.

Wesley suddenly stood. "Let's get out of here. She's had enough."

Anna smiled at Stemmons, obviously pleased at the suggestion and started to stand, but Joe flapped a hand, waving Wesley back into his chair.

Slowly, glowering at Marsh, Stemmons acquiesced.

Joe said, "Did he put the handcuffs on you, Anna?" His voice sounded cool, devoid of emotion, and he wondered how such a detached drone could issue from the high decibel screams going on inside him. He felt like hurricane-force winds were ripping round and round in his belly.

He liked her. Maybe he was beginning to like her too much. Caring was costing him his objectivity. She was so bright, funny, less self-absorbed than most career women he knew. She expressed genuine interest in the world outside herself, which was unusual in a today-kind of female. Before they met he had enjoyed experiencing her warmth over the telephone. Later he had grown curious, of course. Coming, he had been eager to meet the exciting, unpredictable woman Lee had described, always suspecting Lee's descriptions featured a female who was too good to be true.

In order to get acquainted with that woman now, he first had to repair injuries inflicted by a madman. He didn't want to do more harm than the culprit had already inflicted on her. There was no way Joe Marsh was the right man for this job. He had no training. No expertise.

Besides that, he hated hearing her story. And he suspected he was going to detest the rest of it even more.

At the same time, he was convinced Dr. Ware was right. She needed to talk about it. That seemed one way for her to purge. Maybe the only way she would be able to get it out so she could put it behind her.

He had not anticipated his own violent responses. He felt belligerent, as if he'd like to cram his fist down somebody's throat and he was caring less and less about whose.

Their verbal exchange had stopped as he waited for her to answer his last question. She seemed uncertain. He prodded her. "The handcuffs were on the pole, Anna, not on you. Is that right?"

For only that brief moment, his voice slipped its controls and he sounded louder, gruffer, angrier than he intended. He needed to insulate her from his anger. He was taking this much too personally.

She looked up quickly, startled either by his volume or his intensity or his determination to have an answer.

"No, they were not on me." She sighed deeply and refused to raise her eyes to his as she mumbled. "Not then anyway."

Marsh took a sip of beer to kill the bile reflux in his mouth before he continued. "You were afraid of the pole and the handcuffs?"

She nodded without looking up.

"Did you consider you might be able to use the handcuffs as a weapon or a tool to help you escape?"

Her eyes shot to his face and he could see wetness shimmering in the darkened hollows under her eyes. He glanced at Stemmons and saw a similar haunted look in his face. This was difficult for all of them, but she needed to get this poison out. The task was like forcing a child to vomit a contaminate, expel the poison from its system before the toxin inflicted permanent damage.

Like physical poisons, mental pollutants probably should be forced out as quickly as possible after exposure. He didn't know if there was medical research to confirm his theory but it seemed reasonable.

Anna peered into his face. "They were chained to the pole you see."

Yes, he saw. She had drawn a graphic picture, had ably conveyed it from her memory into his brain and he despised the pictures forming there. Still, he thought it entirely appropriate for one friend to share another's most terrifying mental pictures.

He looked at her hands which were suddenly flat, palms down, on the table. He tried to disregard the scarring, the faint, angry red abrasions which he hoped would disappear eventually. He studied instead the long, tapering fingers as they began moving, gracefully rearranging the unused cutlery remaining on the table, creating various designs. He admired the smooth ivory of those delicate hands. He wanted to cover them with his calloused ones, let his absorb any blows delivered against her.

He had followed signaling devices to air crashes and car accidents, had seen people dead and dying, shattered and broken. But those things, all the grotesque physical injuries could be fathomed, eventually accepted by the brain. This damage—buried so deep, invisible—was the unconscionable menace willfully inflicted by a fiend.

No wonder she had refused to talk about it, to return there by recalling memories of the place and the events.

He needed to toughen up to get through it as a voyeur. And he reminded himself again: they hadn't yet gotten to the worst of it. He suddenly felt more determined than before to hear the whole, sordid story, he just wasn't certain if he could handle any more tonight.

He probably should have a session with Dr. Bergin Ware, have the expert help set his course. Marsh's growing regard for the woman was fueling his indignation. Ware might know some tricks to help reduce the pressure on the hearer.

In order to help her, Marsh felt like he needed to distance himself from her, just a little...just for tonight.

Again he looked at her hands, the fine bones in her wrists which should never be encircled by anything other than exquisite bracelets. What sane man would even consider putting those delicate wrists in shackles?

He raised his eyes to her pert chin, her generous mouth, her aristocratic nose, the almond-shaped eyes which so often tonight had shimmered with unindulged tears, alert, dark eyes which recorded and grasped things quickly; the dark, expressive brows which so ably reflected her moods.

Maybe he only imagined the depth, the sensitivity he saw in her, and the silent promise of a full, rich vein of passion that might never be mined now because of the stupidity of some neanderthal, a madman who was still free to seize and victimize other lovely young women.

Stemmons was right. They needed to call it a night.

Marsh stood casually and put his hand on the back of her chair, indicating he was ready to leave. She looked surprised, but stood.

He didn't move out of her path, but braced himself and presented his open hands to her, waist high. She frowned up at him.

"Will you let me hold you?" he asked solemnly.

Her eyes rounded and she shivered but her voice was firm. "No."

"Do you mean no, as in not right now?"

"Yes."

"But you are going to let me hold you eventually, aren't you?"

She regarded his hands. He bobbed his head up and down, indicating she should put her hands on his. Her fingers trembled as she set her palms over his. He held steady and, gradually, she seemed to absorb his calm. Not only did her hands stop their incessant shaking, they warmed.

Someday, maybe, if the scars in her psyche healed, she might be free again to give and receive pleasure from a man—the right man.

Her innocence and sweetness drew him to her. The chime of her laughter earlier, at the apartment, had charmed him. He found pleasure in her energy and even in the now-wary enthusiasm for people and life.

Before this was over, Marsh promised himself, he would find the man who had done this to her. And the son-of-a-bitch would pay beyond what the laws of a civilized society required. Marsh would collect a portion of this debt with his own two hands. It would be revenge, pure and true. That kind of retribution might be the only thing to sate the gnawing helplessness he felt at this moment.

The law could have him when Marsh was finished, but he intended to collect Anna's pound of flesh first, and keep collecting it until she pronounced it enough.

First, however, he'd have the whole, ugly story. But he wouldn't push too hard, not for any of their sakes. He didn't want to pursue it any more tonight.

And Anna? She didn't need anyone adding to her psychological injuries. If he wanted her to come away from this experience strong, healthy, vibrant again, he'd need some guidance.

Was full recovery possible?

Maybe.

But, first, because she was calmer as they stood there, face to face, in the bustle of the restaurant, a little more vomitus.

"What did you do when you saw the pole and the handcuffs?"

There was a fire in her eyes as they met his. Unexpectedly, she kept her hands on his. "What do you think I did? I screamed. I wrapped the quilt around me, paced every inch of that cage and I yelled my fool head off in every direction." She stood stock still, face to face with him, staring in disbelief.

"The noise of my own screaming frightened me. You cannot even imagine that kind of terror. My screams echoed down the halls, eerily, like the sound of someone running away."

The fire in her eyes cooled. "But no one came." Her voice became soft, even listless. "I screamed myself hoarse. I would quit for a while, until my throat stopped burning, then I would scream some more."

"Did the place where you were held ever get darker or lighter?"

She frowned at him, as if she were seeking the right answer from him or trying to remember.

"Slightly. The glow sometimes dimmed and became darker, sometimes lighter. But it was not like there was day and night. I guess that's why, when I got...back, I didn't know how long I'd been gone. It seemed like weeks. For certain it seemed longer than fifty-three hours."

She shifted her weight from one foot to the other and removed her hands from his. "Please, Joe, could we stop now?"

He didn't remember her calling him by his first name before. He loved the sound of it coming from her lips. He responded slowly, as if his answer required deep thought. It didn't. She could have asked him for anything at that moment and he would have given it. Anything.

He smiled. Moving deliberately, he tried to clasp her hand. She withdrew it beyond his grasp. He waited, his open hand poised, suspended where hers had been.

Grimacing, she pushed her hand closer to his and stiffened, as if offering a blood sacrifice. Without grasping her hand, he brushed his thumb over her knuckles.

She bit her bottom lip and lowered her gaze to their hands. Hers quaked, but she didn't withdraw it.

He thought her enigmatic smile was genuine relief as he turned away, allowing her to follow unencumbered.

Chapter Eight

"I knew you were the man." Wesley Stemmons crowed, repeating the mantra over and over, emphasizing different words, as he drove the two of them to his apartment after dropping Anna at her place. "I knew you could get her back for me."

Getting her back for Stemmons? Now there was a reach. But Marsh didn't say that. "She's not back yet."

"Yeah, but you gonna do it, my man, bring her right back around to her old self. And I'm not the only one gonna be thanking you for that. Everyone likes Anna, Joe. No one who knew her before likes her being like this. We've all been grieving over it."

"What about the cops, Wes? Are they following up on the investigation?"

Stemmons shook his head, keeping his eyes on the road. "They might be if they had the information you dragged out of her tonight. That'd be a big help, if they knew it."

"So you'll pass the word, right?"

Wesley studied the road curiously. "Nah. If she wants 'em to know, she can tell 'em."

"Lee..."

"She wouldn't give it up before, don't you see? Kept saying she didn't remember. It wasn't that she *couldn't*. She *wouldn't*. That made 'em suspicious of her. See what I'm getting at?"

Joe stared at Wesley, stunned. "Suspicious about what?"

"I don't know. You know cops, they see too much evil, too many kinky folks. They get to thinking perverse is more normal than normal is normal, if you get my meaning."

Joe cut his gaze to the side window, ignoring Lee's implication. He watched the passing view—the darkened buildings. When he spoke, his words were quiet, as if he were talking to himself. "It sounds like a basement in a commercial building. The humming machine sound is probably the power plant. But where? Which one?"

"Someplace downtown, you figure?"

"I don't think so. I think it's on campus. She was there when she was abducted, and at Duck Pond Park, half a block off campus, when they found her."

Wesley didn't look at Marsh as he asked the question. "Do you think he...? You know, stripping her and all, do you think he...?"

"I can't figure any reason he'd take her clothes unless he had something like that in mind." Joe gave his companion an accusing look. "You're the one who assured me she hadn't been sexually molested."

"Yeah, and that was what they told me, as far as it went. But I was thinking they might not be able to tell all that well, if she'd...ah...well...if she'd like...cooperated."

Marsh's temper spiked. "What the hell kind of friend are you, Stemmons?"

Wesley's hands tightened on the steering wheel. He kept his eyes on the road. "I didn't mean nothing, man, but you know women."

"I don't know *this* woman and, from what you've said so far, it doesn't sound like you've had the opportunity to *know* her either, in the biblical sense. How about if we give her the benefit of the doubt until some evidence persuades us otherwise?"

Looking at Lee's injured countenance, Marsh swallowed his quick anger. "She opened up with us tonight, buddy. It was good. It eased the pressure off of her some. I imagine we'll get to the sexual part sooner or later, if we keep prying." Joe kept an eye on his friend. "The thing I'm worried about is how *we*'ll take it when we get there—you or me either. We have to pursue this for her sake. It's festered long enough. What we've got to do is lance this mental abscess, cut the poison out and put that sweet thing back right."

Joe was thoughtful several minutes before he spoke again. "Your shrink friend, what'd he say?" Without waiting for Stemmons to answer, he continued. "Of course, Lee, you probably know her a lot better than he does. What kind of read do you get?"

Wesley shook his head. "To hell with the shrinks. We're doing better than the pros did, and we're just following your gut instincts. You're the one getting her to open up." Wesley glowered at the traffic light holding them. "He told me to get her talking and get her into therapy, if I had any influence at all. That Doc Ware is supposed to be good. People told him I could talk her into seeing him, but I couldn't. That don't mean you can't."

Joe detected a note of bitterness in the comment. "Don't start getting confused about this, Lee. You called me, remember. You're the one who insisted I come."

"I don't remember you complaining. Besides, I called you for her sake, not for mine...or for yours. Keep that in mind, good buddy."

"Okay. A brick wall doesn't have to fall on me. You've made it clear you want her for yourself." Marsh shook his head. "I still can't see that happening. You, attitude-wise, the blackest black man I've ever known, chasing a white woman."

Wesley frowned at the street. "I can't explain it either, man, not even to myself." He paused for a long, thoughtful moment. "Like most white women, she's probably not much good in the sack, probably don't give herself over to the enjoyment of the deed."

Marsh managed a wry grin. "That's exactly the bad black attitude I'm talking about. You're some kind of a black chauvinist, man, bragging, perpetuating the old line: 'Once you've had black, you'll never go back.'"

Joe grinned as he realized he was picking up a rap beat as he talked. "That's crap, man. White folks romp just as hard 'tween the sheets as black folks do."

Wesley hawked a phony laugh. "Do you know that for fact, or are you just wishing, white bread? You ever had black?"

"That's a very personal question, friend, and you and I ain't that close."

"The answer's no, then." Lee squinted at him. "Am I right?"

"To tell you the truth, I'm not exactly sure."

"I see. Well, consider this: a black woman passing might have it in her head not to enjoy it so much, thinking to make her act more convincing."

"I guess it could happen like that. You ever had white?"

Wesley flashed a rueful glance. "Like you said, Marsh, we ain't that close."

Both men allowed hollow laughs before Marsh focused a harsh stare on the driver. "So, what makes you think Anna would be any different than any other uptight white woman?"

Wesley didn't respond as he negotiated an exit around cones marking road construction. "Because with her, Marsh, I wouldn't care. I'd give her everything I had and keep on giving until she was satisfied, one way or another. Then I'd use whatever I learned to keep making her happy, whatever it took. Bodies are easy. I can make her body happy. It's her soul I'm looking to own."

Joe grinned in disbelief. "Because you think she's got a black gospel singer's soul in that white woman's body? Maybe I do understand. She does get under a man's skin, black or white." He snorted a derisive laugh which seemed to mock them both.

"You're worse than I remember, Marsh. Even your subconscious is doing that punning thing now. You have heard that's the lowest form of humor, haven't you? For a guy with your education, it's downright revolting."

Marsh rewarded the observation with a plastic smile.

They drove in silence the rest of the way to Wesley's apartment where their moods remained reflective and subdued.

Wesley listened to messages on his answering machine while Marsh folded out the sofa bed in the living room and peeled down to his boxers.

"You still lifting weights regular?" Wesley's studied gaze did not make his guest uncomfortable.

"Yeah. And I jog most mornings. I try to stay in some kind of shape. How about you?"

"Even when I do, I don't get those results."

Marsh smiled sympathetically. "Nothing wrong with your physique. Tall as you are, you might could carry a little more meat. Me, I'm fighting my weight all the time. I'd like someone to tell me to put on eight or ten pounds. I could probably do it in a day."

Both men laughed easily as Wesley went to his room, returned with the extra pillow and threw it, catching Marsh in the side of the head. Joe turned a frown on his host, then gave up another grin. He probably deserved at least one wallop upside the head.

Chapter Nine

Marsh dreamed of Anna—provocative dreams—and woke up eager to see her again. But first he intended to talk to Dr. Ware.

At eight he called the man's office to see what time he could stop by.

The receptionist laughed. "Doctor isn't seeing new patients. He has no openings, even for his regular patients, for the next seven weeks, unless it's an emergency. Even then, it had better be for real."

"I think he'll want to talk to me. Why don't you ask him."

"He's with a patient."

"I'll hold."

"I'm afraid it will be quite a wait."

"That's okay. Tell him my name's Joe Marsh and I'm working with Anna Fulenweider. I'm a friend of hers. I think he'll be interested."

He held two or three minutes before Dr. Ware came on the line. The analyst immediately agreed to clear some time. Could he be at Ware's office by 9:30?

"You bet."

After Marsh introduced himself and they shook hands, sizing each other up, he and Ware settled in the doctor's office which looked to Joe more like a comfortable study in someone's home.

Sixtyish, Ware was a stout little man whose stoop made him look smaller than he was, but his eyes were alert, and Joe knew it would be easy to underestimate the man.

When the preliminaries about the weather and parking difficulties around the building had been covered, Ware settled deeper into his chair and lit a pipe as if he could give this conversation all the time in the world. Marsh couldn't remember the last time he'd seen anyone smoke a pipe. He liked the smell.

When the pipe tobacco had begun to glow as Ware pulled on it, the doctor said, "How is Anna?"

Joe gave him a quick report of his initial conversations with Anna, detailing their words but omitting the scenes. He described her behavior and her responses to various subjects, gestures, and other stimuli.

"The problem is, doc, I don't know what I'm doing. What if I mess up and compound the damage that's already been done?"

Ware laid his pipe in an ashtray and flipped through pages in a file propped in his lap.

"Joe, I believe Anna's problems," Ware said, "are exacerbated by her keeping them bottled up." His piercing eyes suddenly locked with Marsh's. "You are the fellow from Colorado, is that correct?"

"Yes."

"Then you have an advantage starting out. She trusts you. Now, how personally involved are you with her?"

"I met her for the first time yesterday morning."

"Aren't you the one she'd interviewed about the tracking apparatus?"

"Yes, but those interviews were by telephone. Long distance."

"She spoke as if she knew you."

Marsh thought Anna had refused to speak with Ware. As they talked, he was surprised that the doctor seemed to know so much about him.

"I didn't know she'd talked to you."

"We had a couple of sessions, although I did most of the talking. That is not the way it's supposed to work in my business. I am a generation older than Anna, Joe, and I'm a happily married man, but even I was impressed. She is a delightful young woman with wonderful powers of observation. Do you find her attractive?"

"Well, sure. Any man would. She's real pretty and sexy, too, in kind of a wholesome way, if you know what I mean. But...to tell you the truth, it looks to me like she's damaged goods."

He caught Ware's scowl of disapproval out of the corner of his eyes and didn't attempt a direct look at the older man. "Do you know about the shakes and about her not letting anyone touch her?" Joe asked, attempting to cover the awkward moment. He was aware of movement as the older man nodded solemnly and lowered his eyes again to the pages in the file in front of him.

"Yes," Ware said after a long delay. "She may have a long road to travel before she's well. And she's going to need some help along the way from her friends." He nailed Marsh with what appeared to be an accusing glance. "It may be a while before she's strong enough to handle some eager beaver's sexual appetite." He continued the disapproving glower.

Joe suddenly felt defensive, as if he were being warned. "I realize that."

"Any man who is sincerely interested in her will have to put any romantic illusions on hold, if he expects to help her." The doctor hesitated and dropped the stoney glare. "I doubt you're that man."

"You don't know anything about me or what kind of man I am. You may be an good analyst, but you're jumping the gun pigeonholing me."

"Are you that interested in her welfare?" Ware looked indifferent.

"I don't know how interested *that* interested is."

"Enough to exercise some self discipline, to control one's appetites, to set aside normal hormonal urgings."

"I'm no animal, doc, if that's what you want to know."

"She has to be able to trust someone, preferably a man." The doctor sounded vaguely disappointed. "I hoped it would be me but, unfortunately, we don't get to dictate who others choose to trust. You are the one she apparently has picked, at least for the moment."

"Yeah." Joe liked the sound of that and smiled. "Also, I think she likes me a little, too."

Ware turned a harsh stare on Marsh. "Is that to say you think she might be attracted to you?"

Joe didn't want to sound immodest, but he was trying to be candid. "Yes, sir, but there's a glitch in that part of it."

"Stemmons?"

"How did you know?"

"It's obvious to anyone who's seen them together."

Wanting to couch his amateur interference in her psychological problems in the best light, at the same time equally determined to give Ware the facts, Joe described how he and Anna met, including Wesley's part, the compromising circumstances, which he had omitted before; the car drive and the events at her condominium.

"Wesley and I took her out to dinner last night."

"Probably a good idea," Ware interjected, speaking for the first time in several minutes of Joe's narrative. "Safety in numbers and all that."

"Yes, well, we had a couple of beers and she opened up some."

"Did you force it?"

"No, not exactly, but I did nudge her pretty hard a couple of times."

Ware cleared his throat, which sounded like the prelude to a rebuke and Marsh hurried on. "Like I told you before, she seemed to get some relief from talking about it. I thought that was a step in the right direction. But I didn't know what I was doing—just going with my intuition like that—and I sure don't want to screw things up or do her any harm."

He could practically hear the gears in the doctor's brain grinding before Ware seemed to reach some kind of compromise with himself. "All right, Marsh. Let's do it this way. I will advise you and we will map our strategy as we go. You may prod her along, but take it easy. The main thing for you to remember is not to comment on anything she tells you. Don't offer suggestions about what she might have done differently compared to what she did do. Hindsight's 20/20, you know."

Marsh winced at the cliché. "I've heard."

"You're right in realizing she needs to talk about it." He regarded Marsh skeptically. "I'd feel a lot better about this if you could convince her to do her talking to me, but failing that, this will have to do for now, unless..."

"What?"

"You need to stop immediately if you begin to judge her, to dislike her for past events or behavior. She'll feel that judgment and that might shove her right back into that black hole of depression. Do you understand?"

"Yes."

"And whatever you do, don't force her."

Marsh hesitated under the power of the doctor's stare. "That's where I'm most afraid of making a mistake, doc. She was stubborn at first. I had to push her pretty hard to get her talking. I don't want to cross over some invisible line and make matters worse."

"In a case like this," Ware sounded as if he were choosing his words carefully, "the victim is ashamed, has usually convinced herself she somehow initiated or at least contributed to her situation. That self-condemnation is rarely justified, even in the farthest stretches of the imagination, but a relatively innocent person has a hard time believing a bad guy can be as perverse as he is without some kind of invitation from his victim.

"If you can, encourage her to tell her story the way she sees it. Don't try to lead her or give her any indication of what you'd like the story to be. If you do, she might be tempted to change it to accommodate you. We need her to air what she thinks happened. Manipulating her to confess what you think happened won't help her.

"Once you get her talking, if she stammers or hesitates, you wait. Don't try to fill in any gaps. Let it come from her.

"Most importantly, for God's sake, man, don't react. Don't show any emotion at all, no approval, no disapproval, no anger, nothing. Don't express pleasure or disappointment in anything you hear. Don't get angry. Be objective. Can you do that?"

Marsh gave him a wary look. "I've already tipped my hand some, but I couldn't help it. Hell, I wanted to kill the S.O.B. with my bare hands. I can't stand to think about how he treated her, unless, right along with it, I imagine torturing him for it. That seems like the only way I can cope."

Ware shook his head and studied his pipe resting in the ashtray, but didn't pick it up. "It may get worse before you see light at the end of the tunnel."

"What do you think I'm going to hear?"

Ware raised his eyes to stare at Joe a long moment before he spoke, his voice quiet. "She may have been forced to...well, to perform what she considers perverse acts."

"Sexual acts?"

"Maybe. It could be behavior you or I might not consider particularly bad but which she considers unforgivable. I have the impression that Ms. Fulenweider does not have a lot of experience on which to base these judgments."

Marsh stared behind Ware wondering at his own response. He thought Anna might still have been a virgin, at least before the pervert got hold of her. To be honest, he didn't know how much more of her story he could hear without blowing up. But he didn't want to shake Ware's fledgling confidence in him.

"I can try."

"The main thing to remember is, you are the one who has her confidence. It is in everybody's best interest for you to sustain that confidence. You must keep everything she tells you inviolate, absolutely secret."

"But I don't know what I'm doing. I need to talk to you to get some guidance."

Ware drew a deep breath. "Yes, that's probably true. How about if I agree to make myself available when you need to confide in me. But she's going to be sharing the secrets of her heart, of her innermost self. Except for me, you must keep those secrets in strictest confidence."

"How should I start?"

"Just as you have already. Get her talking. Guide her to the subject. She's a newspaper reporter. She's used to reducing events to words, relaying the most significant information first.

"Or, she may prefer to tell it like it's a fairy tale. Like a fiction that happened to someone else. Or maybe you can encourage her to begin at the beginning and reel the events out to you in chronological order. If she gets stuck, you can jump ahead and come back to the sticky part later. What I recommend you do, Marsh, is whatever works. Feel your way carefully."

Joe uncrossed his legs and prepared to stand, thinking the consultation must be over, but Ware wasn't through.

"I cannot stress strongly enough that you must not consider your own feelings in the equation." The doctor peered sternly into Joe's face. "Act strictly as a sounding board. Do not allow yourself to make any judgments. Do not show approval or disapproval. Can you do that?"

"Like I said, I can try."

"You respect Anna, don't you, Marsh?"

"Yes, I do."

"That will help. Nurture that regard. Make a mental list of her attributes and refer back to them when you are tempted to judge her too harshly."

Marsh smiled. He'd spent half the night reviewing Anna Fulenweider's attributes. That would definitely be the easy part of this assignment.

"I need to see her alone." Marsh regarded Wesley skeptically. "I think I can get her to open up more if things are calm and there're no other people around, or distractions."

Stemmons didn't return Marsh's look as he tied a half Windsor knot in the necktie, leaving the length underneath short. He frowned his disapproval, but didn't rework the knot. "Don't be hustling her."

Joe flashed him a mischievous, non-threatening grin.

But Stemmons was not in a kidding mood. "I mean it, man. You've got a reputation with the ladies, but she's too vulnerable, wearing her feelings right out in the open like she is. You can't get her all shivery wanting you and leave 'er. She's gotta be handled with care, not like another notch on your pistol. I don't want you leaving her worse off than you found her. 'You hear?"

Marsh didn't appreciate the threat, but knew Anna wasn't the only one wearing her heart on her sleeve. He had to follow Ware's instructions, tiptoe around the woman's sensitivities. No one would expect him to be sensitive to Wesley's feelings as well, but he would try.

"Look, man, you sent for me." He repeated the reminder. "What have you got that's working better?"

Wesley turned a harsh glare on his guest, as if sizing him up.

Three inches taller, Lee was slim compared to Marsh's muscular girth, yet on this subject, he obviously did not intend to be intimidated.

"I mean it, Joe. This is no game. No competition. No macho bragging rights go with laying her."

Marsh had been sitting on the side of the bed watching Stemmons try to rework the tie. Suddenly he stood, ran his thumbs around his belt line, easing wrinkles out of his shirt where it pleated itself into his slacks.

"I'm just as serious as you are, Lee. You've got to give me some operating room. I need to experiment, find what levers move us forward, which of her buttons run what. I can't be worrying if something that works is going to offend you. Now, do you want me to try, using any tools that get the job done, or don't you?"

Wesley looked hard at Marsh's reflection in the mirror. "Don't make her worse."

Shaking his head, Joe's gaze caught and held Wesley's as he felt himself softening. "I'm not a trained analyst, Lee. I don't know what psychological bombshells the perp may have set..."

"No mechanisms."

Joe gritted his teeth. "We don't know that because we don't know yet what makes her tick. That's what I'm going to try to find out first."

"What do you mean?" Wesley stopped fumbling with the necktie.

"Did she have sex with him?"

"Doctor said not."

"I want to hear it from her. He did something, touched her inappropriately, something. Personally, I think he molested her and in some way, she blames herself. I don't know where else all that guilt could be coming from. Do you?"

Stemmons whipped around and took a threatening step toward Marsh, balling his fists. "Hell, why would she be thinking she's guilty of anything? Is that trash coming out of your own sick mind?"

Marsh thought it best not to tell Lee he was confiding in Ware. "I've been reading, Lee. Women sometimes blame themselves for being assaulted, think something they did—sexy clothes they wore, putting themselves in a compromising place, a smile, something—contributed to the perp's behavior. Sometimes they hate themselves for cooperating enough to save their own lives."

"No." Wesley's jaws clenched and he shook his head, as if trying to shake the mental pictures out his mind. "She knows better than that. Nobody's thinking she encouraged him."

Marsh puckered his lips and kept a watchful eye on his friend. Stemmons sure was having a hard time with this. "Lee, what I'm trying to say is, you can't tie my hands. I like her. I like you. I'll try not to get in the way of your moving on her, but you're going to have to cut me some slack. Give me room to maneuver."

"Like what are you thinking?" Wesley obviously didn't like the idea of giving Marsh carte blanche.

"She trusts me. We need to develop a stronger rapport. To do that, we're going to have to spend time together, grow some mutual respect. Bond. And we'll have to do that without you glaring at us, interrupting at crucial moments, criticizing my words or methods. See what I mean?"

Stemmons bit back whatever he started to say in rebuttal and bowed his head. He was silent for several heartbeats before squaring his shoulders. His voice was low. "I need to tell you something you don't know. This is my fault. Marsh, I wanted her so damn bad..." He muttered some unintelligible words, then hesitated.

"Lee, we don't need any more guilt in this little melodrama than we've already got. What are you trying to take blame for here? That you called me or that she showed up at the pageant early?"

Shaking his head, Stemmons picked his billfold up off the dresser, shoved it in a back pocket, scooped up a set of keys and a handful of change, dropping those items in a front pocket.

Meticulously, he folded two tissues and slid those into the other front pocket. He picked up a second set of keys, obviously car keys, which he tossed to Marsh who one-handed them out of the air.

Wesley said, "You can drive me to work and keep my car. Do what's right but," he flashed a cautioning look, "let your conscience be your guide." He stepped close. "And consult your conscience before you make any moves on her because I'm gonna expect detailed reports, and I damn well expect to cross examine you to pick up on any ulterior motives." He cast a significant glance at the zipper on Joe's trousers. "Am I coming through clear about that?"

Marsh rolled the car keys in his hand, gazing at them. "Loud and clear."

Chapter Ten

Joe drove. As agreed, the men picked up Anna at her condo on their way to the office.

"Anna, Joe's going to hang with you today," Wesley said casually as they rode downtown.

Situated between them, after another losing skirmish over seating, Anna stared straight ahead. "Why?"

Wesley's arm rested on the back of the seat behind her. If she noticed, she didn't object.

"Because he'll be in my way in the lab and I've got work to do. There's more space for him to hang out with you in the newsroom."

She seemed satisfied with that explanation.

As Marsh wheeled into the parking lot, a student intern, Lela Jamison bumped the passenger door. Wesley lowered the window and she thrust a set of car keys at Anna.

"Dollar Hardware's on fire. We picked it up off the scanner. It's five alarm, flames are all the way into the apartments on the seventh floor. Go, go, go."

Wesley held up a hand, staying Marsh for a minute, then reached across Anna to turn the key and kill the engine before he bailed out the passenger door. "You two take the company car. I've gotta get my wide-angle from the darkroom. I'll drive this and meet you there."

With no other conversation, Marsh exited the driver's door and trailed Anna as she sprinted across the parking lot. When she reached an aged Seville, she clamored inside.

"Want me to drive?" Marsh said, pausing only long enough to ask.

"You don't know the way. Get in. Hurry or you don't go."

He took her at her word and leaped around, scrambling into the passenger seat as the car sputtered to life.

"A Cadillac's pretty spiffy for a staff car, don't you think?" He marveled at her driving as she blared through slower traffic, weaving, veering.

He gave her one thing, she had a good eye for space as she shot through what appeared to him to be inadequate openings, and got within a whisper of other vulnerable fenders with nearly every maneuver.

"It's twelve years old and has nearly two hundred thousand miles on it. We're the last hurrah for this old geezer."

He heard the affection in her voice and he smiled. This woman was going to take some serious sorting out.

Anna was not beautiful in the usual way, Marsh decided, eying her critically in his effort to keep his mind off the multiple close brushes with disaster as she accelerated and braked, crisscrossing traffic lanes.

There was almost a dreamlike quality about her. Her dark eyes slanted giving them almost a Polynesian cast. Her mouth was overly large and her chin a little short. Yet, the combination pulled him like a magnet.

For all of her bravado, there was something very feminine about Anna, a womanly essence, untapped; and joy, optimism she seemed careful to keep suppressed. He intended to mine that prize vein all the way down to the mother lode, which he imagined was buried deep inside her lovely, enigmatic shell.

She was going to tell him her whole story and much more. He might have to bully it out of her. He would go easy, of course, like Ware said. He smiled at his own quandary. He might enjoy this little adventure more than he had imagined.

People scurried like ants as the Seville neared the scene of the fire. Anna had to park a block away. They jumped out and ran, their strides in sync. Joe couldn't help marveling at how well they moved together.

They ran side-by-side to the line of police barricading the inferno which roared and belched clouds of thick, black smoke, corrupting the clear morning sky. Bits of black ash drifted back like lazy snowflakes, dusting everything and everyone below.

Police busily rerouted traffic on the street siding the besieged building. Cars parked at the curbing on both sides of the street appeared they would be directly in the crash zone, if the building's side wall collapsed.

Joe watched a patrolman use a tire iron to break a wing window in an older model pickup truck. The uniformed officer reached through to unlock the door, threw it open, hopped inside and crammed the gearshift into neutral. He stretched a leg, trying to push the vehicle and steer it at the same time.

Marsh glanced at Anna, who had wormed her way inside the barricade and was scribbling in her notebook. Then he looked back at the patrolman struggling to move the truck. Without a word, Joe ran to the back of the truck to push. Another civilian stepped up to join the effort.

They shoved the pickup around a corner, into an alley but the patrolman yelled for them to keep pushing until they were nearly a full block from the fire.

"Why'd we take it so far?" the other civilian asked.

They followed the patrolman who ran, returning to the vehicles still on the street. "To leave room for more. As many as we can get."

It was a plan. Primitive, but it would do. The patrolman passed up two newer model cars for an older one.

"Why not these?" The other civilian paused a moment beside each of those by-passed.

The patrolman shouted to be heard above the noise of men yelling, motors humming as the traffic jam of fire trucks pumped water to the blaze, and the roar of the fire itself as flames shot what seemed like obscene gestures at the opposing army of firefighters.

"Steering wheels lock on those when the motor's off. Gotta have ignition keys. We don't have 'em."

Joe glanced around to locate Anna. She stood beside the man wearing the fire chief insignia, still scribbling in the notebook. She looked safe enough. He turned to find his team tackling another stranded vehicle and raced to join them as they coaxed a convertible from its parking place and around the corner. They rammed it close behind the pickup truck.

They rescued another, then another. Each time, Joe scanned until he found Anna: speaking with a man with a manager's badge on his shirt; listening to a bald round fellow who resembled Santa out-of-season, and other bystanders. Joe wasn't particularly concerned for her safety, he just liked keeping tabs on her. And each time his eyes actually found her, he got a fresh jolt of adrenaline for the physical demands.

Marsh and his impromptu team of car-jackers were returning down the alley toward the fire when they heard a series of loud pops and cracks, then an ominous rumbling. Standing safely out of its path, they watched the wall crumple and buckle before it exploded into the street, crushing the cars which remained parked at the curbs, the ones they hadn't had the time or the tools to move.

Firemen shouted and ran, diverting two hoses from the building to the rubble in the street. From the far side of the commotion, Marsh heard enhanced shouts, able to decipher only the two most repeated words: "*Chief's down.*"

Obviously someone thought the fire chief was trapped beneath the smoldering debris. Joe hesitated. There were plenty of trained men wearing the right equipment to dig out their commander. His most immediate concern was Anna.

She had been standing with the chief earlier, but had moved along. Still, Joe chilled at the thought she might have sought the commander out once more for an update.

Marsh scanned the onlookers but it was difficult to discern shapes, much less faces, through the smoke and dust and steam rising off the remains of the building barricading the street, barring his return.

Turning, he ran down the alley, out the far end, around the block and back, but patrolmen manning the taped perimeter stopped him.

"I've got to get in there." He shouted, trying to convince the patrolman to let him through. He was getting nowhere and had about decided to throw a punch to get the guy out of his way when the patrolman he'd helped with the cars ran up beside him, breathless. "He's with...with me."

"He shoulda' said so." The unreasoning guard gave Marsh a grudging look, then raised the tape to allow both Marsh and his teammate to pass.

"Thanks," Joe rasped at the patrolman.

"What's up?"

Marsh studied the crowd of firefighters and rescue workers, including two figures occupying stretchers near the ambulance. She wasn't there. "I've gotta find someone. She was just here."

"Marsh?"

He turned at the sound of her voice and his breath caught in his throat.

She stood about twenty feet away, dusted with fine black soot and ash, but she was upright and appeared to be sound. When his eyes reached her face, however, her features were distorted with what looked like pain. A dozen quick steps and he stood directly in front of her. "Are you hurt?"

She shook her head. "I saw you over there." She pointed toward the street which had vanished beneath the collapsed wall, "moving cars. I..."

"What?"

"When the wall fell, I thought you were there. I thought you..." The rest of her thought created tears which pooled in her eyes then became rivulets that traced through the soot and etched wavering tracks down her face.

Marsh stood astonished for a moment, before an involuntary response opened his arms. She shuffled forward, sniffing, swiping at the tears, smudging her pale skin, giving it the look of some ghoulish finger-painting. He didn't know if she realized what she was doing as she walked straight into his arms. He didn't want to alarm her, so he closed them around her gently, not knowing how she might react when she realized what she had done.

He glanced up. His patrolman pal studied him for a long moment, then gave a quick wave, and took his place on the taped perimeter.

Anna felt smaller in his arms than Joe had expected, fragile cocooned against his body. He drew a deep breath, oblivious to the commotion going on around them, and raised his chin enough to rest it on her head. She settled as if she belonged there. Surprisingly, he realized: she did.

The tender moment didn't last nearly long enough. He was aware the second she became conscious of their unusual circumstance, because she stiffened and shot her head up, clipping his chin. Accusation flashed in her eyes.

He relaxed his arms to exonerate himself, but didn't release her completely, keeping his hands on her upper arms. "You came to me, baby. You needed holding. I only reacted. I didn't start it." He wanted to establish the blame before she began to hurl a lot of false accusations they both would know were not true.

She backed two steps, stammering, unable to find the right words. He decided to help.

"I'm glad you didn't want a wall to fall on me. I think that shows improvement in our relationship."

Her eyes sparked. "We have no *relationship*, Marsh."

He gave her a smug smile. "Oh, yes, we do, sweetheart. And it's just going to keep getting better and better."

She bit her lips and the almond eyes rounded. She glowered at him a long minute. Then, magically, her shoulders relaxed and her expression softened. "Got me again, didn't you?"

"Teasing you is one of the perks of the job."

A slow smile slipped across her soot-muddied face, dazzling, hitting him like spontaneous combustion, lighting him up inside. Obviously that smile was a smattering of what Wesley had described, the contagious joy she had radiated before. Joe could see it now, the sparkle that could turn a strong man wrong side out, have him head over heels in a heartbeat. Grab a root, Joe, he cautioned himself, you're starting to spin.

He returned the smile with a grin calculated to reassure her. He didn't want her to see the effect she had on him. It'd give her too much of an edge if she knew she could disable him so easily. No, no. He had to stay cool, be the unaffected friend, in spite of the burn her winsome smile ignited. He needed to coax her along, not cave at the first sign of warming.

Besides, this was not some cute little gal signaling a quick tumble and out. No, this was a long-term kind of woman and he was *not* a long-term kind of man. Long-term had never been his style.

Then, too, he had to remember Wesley, his friend with the heart on his sleeve.

Studying her smile, recalling the scent of her, the warmth, the delicate feel of her, Marsh wallowed for a moment in the joy of a peculiar rush.

A man could change his style. It happened.

But could he betray a friend?

That happened, too. And too often, treachery between friends involved a long-term kind of woman.

Chapter Eleven

Marsh was first to shake free of those brief, intimate moments of bonding. She seemed sensitive to his effort to pull away and she withdrew as well. He didn't like the invisible wall he felt slide into place between them.

He covered the awkward moment by saying, "You need to wash your face."

She ran her fingers over the smudged soot which probably felt gritty, and nodded. "Let's go back to the paper. We can clean up and I can get my story down." She glanced at her watch, wheeled, jogged to the taped barriers, ducked under and darted down the street toward the car.

It took Marsh a minute to realize what she meant. She was on deadline. He could keep up or find himself looking for a ride.

Beyond the tape, he broke into a trot, keeping her bobbing figure in sight and cutting the distance between them as she ran to the aged Seville. He thought he had more time, didn't expect the vehicle to start on the first crank, but it did. He grabbed the door handle and leaped inside as the car began rolling. "Couldn't wait?"

"I'm past deadline now. They're holding the presses for my story."

"I didn't see Wesley. Didn't he make it?"

"He was there, all of about ten minutes. He asked me to ride back with him."

"And?"

"I had to find you."

"I wasn't there to slow you down. Don't ever think you have to wait on me. When you need to go, go. I'll manage."

She tossed him a quick glance. "The wall fell. Wesley caught a couple of shots and ran."

"See, he wasn't worried about me."

"He hadn't seen you over there. I didn't mention it. I didn't want to slow him down. Now shut up, I'm trying to think my lead, get the story lined out in my head."

She had hung around, waited to find him, to make sure he was all right. She cared. But she didn't want him to know it. Or maybe she didn't want to admit it to herself. Marsh was quiet a while before he said, "Thanks."

She looked at him as if she were startled, then flashed that million-dollar smile. "You're welcome." The smile vanished as quickly as it had come, replaced by a renewed squint of concentration.

Emerging from the men's room, Marsh felt like doing cartwheels, warmed as he was by a grand feeling of well-being. Anna was at her desk pounding the keyboard.

After drawing another quenching look at her, Joe sauntered to the elevator beyond the editorial department and smiled to himself. He'd seen vending machines in a hallway off the lobby downstairs. He'd get them a can of pop, maybe a candy bar.

She liked him. He didn't know exactly why that was such a big deal. A lot of women liked him. He was a handsome guy, made nice money, didn't carry a bunch of emotional baggage from failed marriages and random hatches of kids. What was not to like?

Yeah, Anna liked him. That knowledge was more significant than any other woman's approval had been...maybe ever.

The only flaw in this developing scenario was Wesley.

Lee obviously was trading on their friendship, his and Joe's, at the same time trying to muster a little sympathy from both his pals to keep himself in the picture.

"No way, buddy." Joe whispered to himself as he tired of waiting for the elevator. He slipped through a door marked "Stairs," and jogged down the stairwell.

Anna was special. Beyond friendship. No, he was declaring this competition open and Contender Joe Marsh was signing up to beat out all comers and take home the trophy. The best man had decided to win.

He flung open a door at the bottom of the stairwell expecting to see the first-floor lobby. Instead, he found himself in a basement.

Apparently, in his reverie, he'd gone a level too far. Not paying enough attention. He was closing the door and turning back to the stairs when a distinctive sound, an engine's hum, caught his attention, piquing his curiosity.

The building's power plant must be there in the basement. This structure apparently had been built before architects conceived the idea of using under-building space for parking.

Marsh shoved the closing door open again and walked into the dimly lighted cavern.

It smelled damp, the familiar odor of wet concrete. The walls were gray, unpainted cement. Lone bulbs provided the only light. Marsh's butt tingled and he recognized the symptom. This might not be *the* place, but it had all the earmarks of being strikingly similar to the prison Anna had described, minus the skylight maybe.

He paced through the open area, noting the huge ventilator pipes, like ones she had said snaked their way along the ceiling of the location where she was held.

Weight-bearing poles gave the space its form, stalwarts standing at attention like a line of tall, silent, steel soldiers awaiting orders.

The drone of a large motor reverberated off the walls and floor and ceiling. A person might get used to it—white noise—eventually be able to sleep in spite of it, but he didn't think the sound could ever qualify in his thinking as what she'd termed *companionable*.

A chain-link cage secured massive heating and cooling units which were the source of the noisy hum.

Underground power plants at the university were probably similar to this one, some even built about the same era, with little thought to utilizing the abundant underground space for parking. Joe would like to see some of those areas under the campus, particularly the ones under the field house and the performing arts center.

Later. Not now, but in a day or two, after she'd opened up a little more, he'd bring her down here, give her a benign look at a place similar to the location of her nightmare, show her she could come and go in and out of this space at will. It would be a good experience for her. He'd be there to guarantee that it was.

He pursed his lips studying the machinery. He'd bring her when she was more stable. And it might not be that long.

"Can you get off this afternoon?" Joe watched her face and was pleased to see she didn't seem adverse to the idea, before a frown crinkled her eyebrows.

"Why?"

"It's seventy degrees outside. We won't have many more days like this before winter weather sets in. How about if you and I go for a walk? I'll bet there's a great city park around here somewhere."

The expressive eyebrows arched and she snorted a laugh. He thought she looked pleased at the prospect. Pay dirt.

The managing editor glanced up, but his eyes stopped at her chest. Marsh did a double take, then took a step forward to see if she had spilled or if there was something particularly eye-catching about the front of her, other than her anatomical attributes at that particular location.

"I'm taking some comp time off this afternoon," she said.

Shifting his gaze to her face, her supervisor nodded and flapped a hand waving her out.

Joe knew he was being overly sensitive to the way men ogled her, but he had valid reasons right now to notice and he added her managing editor to his mental list of suspects. Of course, she should have recognized this guy. Oddly enough, he matched her description of the perp, average height, not exactly pudgy, but could have worn padding to throw her off. Yeah, Joe wasn't letting any potential suspect off without some close scrutiny.

Holed up in his photo lab, Wesley hadn't so much as peeked out to say hello or good-bye. No use bothering him, Marsh figured, as he nudged Anna toward the elevators.

"Did they get any fingerprints?" he asked idly. Multicolored leaves crunched under their footsteps. He liked the way they walked together, in step. He'd reduced the length of his stride just a little to stay in sync with her, pace for pace.

"They might have, if they'd fingerprinted me," she said

"What are you talking about?"

"If they had taken fingerprints off the purloined goods."

"You mean if he had left fingerprints on you? But the patrolman's write-up and the medical reports indicated you weren't...molested. I interpreted that to mean, you weren't touched."

She squeezed her eyes shut and her body language indicated her whole system was shutting down. Then she hissed one word. "Fine."

"Were you?" he prodded.

"Whatever the paperwork says."

"Anna, did the guy touch you...ah...inappropriately?"

She took a deep breath. "Let me ask you, Marsh." Her eyes flashed a warning and he braced himself for a blow—not a physical shot, but a psychological one. "If they had examined the woman who was with you in Wesley's apartment yesterday, would they have been able to determine if she had been sexually assaulted?"

"Yes. And they would have known she hadn't been. We hadn't gotten that far. But that was different. She was willing and you..." The next word caught in his throat.

Anna clamped her lips between her teeth, locked her arms over her chest, ducked her head, and continued walking, outpacing Joe, who lagged behind for a minute to nail down a brand new, renegade thought.

As understanding sluiced through his brain, Joe scowled with unwelcome thoughts and mental pictures before he trotted to catch up with her. "But, why would you have been willing? With him?"

She couldn't seem to speak at first, only waggled her head from side to side, agonizing. Finally, she whispered, "I guess you had to be there."

Marsh clenched his jaws and turned on her before either of them could set up defenses against his unexpected emotional eruption. He didn't know what was happening inside but he felt powerless to stop his own abhorrent rage. Without thinking, he caught her upper arms with both hands and yanked her around to face him. She turned her head to the side, refusing to meet his gaze.

His breathing escalated as he gulped deep draughts of air, trying to regain control, but he was still on the edge when he said, "Look at me, damn it." He shouted the words

pointed at the base. "Was the pole secured? Bolted to the ground like that one, Anna?"

She blinked and backpedaled a step until his hand in the small of her back stopped her retreat.

"It's just a flag pole, Anna. You've seen a hundred just like it. You know there's no evil inherent in this pole, don't you?"

She sniffed. "Sure, but this one doesn't have handcuffs."

Marsh guided Anna to the bench and motioned her to sit.

"Okay, let's start where you woke up on the mattress." He kept talking even after she began shaking her head. "The mattress smelled musty but you said the quilt over you smelled good, like it had been dried in the sunshine."

Grudgingly, she said an affirmative, "Un-huh."

"And?"

"I don't want to talk about this."

"And you don't have to, sweetheart. You only have to tell me about it. No one else."

She grimaced, then, to his surprise, she began speaking again, slowly. "Honestly," she gave him a pleading look. "I tried everything I could think of to get out of there."

How could she possibly think he or anyone else blamed her for being held captive, or for any other part of this debacle? Again, however, he didn't want to interrupt.

"I tried climbing out, but I was barefooted and the wire cut my toes. I kicked and screamed and pried at the locks with my fingers, but there was no way. Then it seemed to get darker."

"Where was the guy?"

"I don't know. He wasn't anywhere where I could see him. Finally, when the shadows were deepest, I heard footsteps.

"I might not have heard them if I'd been sleeping, but I was afraid to sleep. The drone of the machine lulled me and I might have slept, but I was too frightened."

"And you were naked. Are you used to sleeping in the buff?"

"No."

He gave her what he hoped was a kindly smile. "Go on." He had a hard time keeping his mental images under wraps.

"I heard something clink at the gate and I jumped up. I had the quilt around me, but I was ready to fight him and run, clothes or no clothes. I strained trying to see him in the dark, but all I could make out was a form. He was large. Very tall. And heavy. One look and I doubted I'd be able to overpower him but, when I saw how fat he was, I thought I might be able to outrun him.

"Before he opened the gate, he told me to lie down on my stomach with my hands up over my head and lock the handcuffs on my wrists. His voice was only a hiss, definitely male, but a whisper with energy behind it, like he was maybe nervous or excited. I couldn't tell."

"What was he wearing?"

"Sweats...and latex gloves. He was close to the fence and I could tell he wore thick clown makeup all over his face. That frightened me all the more, for him to be dressed like that. He had a shower cap on his head.

"You startled me when you said something about *that clown* a while ago. I wondered how you guessed about that. But, of course, then I realized you didn't know. I have not mentioned that to anyone."

Marsh wanted to keep her on point. "It sounds like the guy was trying to disguise himself. Could he have been someone you know?"

"What I hoped was that he didn't want to have to kill me to keep me from identifying him later." She hesitated. "I thought about that later and it helped me feel better about things, to think he might be intending to let me live."

Marsh looked at her, agreeing without voicing it. "Can you describe his voice?"

"No. When he talked at all, it was always in a whisper, as if there was something wrong with his throat."

"Did he sound like any actor or anyone you know?"

"It's hard to recognize a voice when it has no timbre, when it's only a whisper."

"Then what happened?"

"I said no, I wouldn't put the handcuffs on. He said, 'Do what I say.' I moved back in the cage. I wanted to distract him. I said, 'Who are you? Why are you doing this? Do you want money? I can get you money, if you let me make one phone call.'

"He just repeated, 'Do what I say.'"

"Are you sure it was 'Do what I say,' rather than 'Do as I say' or 'Do like I say.'"

"I'm almost sure."

"Okay, go on."

"I said if he came in there, I would fight him. I told him I'd had self-defense classes, that I knew ways to hurt him even without a weapon."

"How did he react to that?"

"He laughed, but it came out sounding more like a cat, you know, hissing."

She scowled at Marsh, then looked up startled as two kids on inline skates raced down the walk directly in front of their bench. She didn't continue until they were out of earshot.

"I saw the gun, but I didn't actually feel the dart. But I was vaguely aware of it quivering in my arm. Before I could say anything, I was out. I don't even remember hitting the floor."

"Were you unconscious?"

She nodded.

Marsh tried not to appear as concerned as he felt. She would have no way of knowing what that freak had done to her while she was unconscious.

Marsh glanced off in the distance and shifted position but couldn't seem to get comfortable on the bench. He needed to walk some more, try not to let his anger boil up and over again. He stood. "Come on, show me the swimming pool. They've got a municipal pool around here somewhere, haven't they?"

She seemed relieved at the suggestion and rose immediately, dusting the back of her straight, denim skirt. "Yes. It's an Olympic size with a separate diving pool. The local oil company gave it to the city."

"University towns get a lot of perks."

"Yes, Halston attracts a lot of unusual people: gifted, talented, rich people."

"You like it here then?"

"Yes, I do." She hesitated. "Or at least I did."

Chapter Twelve

Joe and Anna walked slowly, smiled at pedestrians coming from the other direction, and lowered their voices when they heard joggers approaching from behind.

"So what happened next?" Marsh said quietly, prodding her again.

Anna shrugged. "Couldn't we just enjoy the day for a while?"

"Later. Now tell me what happened next."

She drew a deep breath. "I was scared to death before I even opened my eyes. I was lying on the mattress on my stomach. My wrists were locked in the handcuffs above my head. The quilt covered me from my neck down.

"Obviously he'd found out about my period. He'd put a rubber sheet under me and he'd left a box of pads and a package with four pairs of bikini panties." She glanced at him. "It was still pretty dark. I couldn't see him from where I was, but I could feel his presence. I knew he was still there, somewhere close.

"He hissed at me. He said, 'You're awake,' or something like that. I didn't say anything. He ran something sharp down the bottom of my foot.

"I pulled my knees up under me, curled into sort of a ball. He shuffled around. I didn't know what he might do. I was frightened.

"Then he squatted down beside me and slipped a key into the cuffs. The spring clip opened and my hands were free. I grabbed the edges of the quilt and wrapped it tightly around me. He'd left the gate open. When I saw that, I tried to jump up, to run, but I was too dizzy or disoriented. He grabbed my arm and pinched me so hard, he made a bruise."

Marsh stared at her, fascinated. "Did he say anything?"

"Yes. He whispered, 'Next time, do what I say.' Then he shoved me. I stumbled and fell on the mattress. He let himself out and stomped off into the darkness.

"I yelled after him. I said I needed tampons."

"How tall was this guy?"

"Average to tall. I'm not real good at proportions but he seemed very tall at first, maybe six-foot-six, but of course, I was on the floor looking up, so he may have appeared taller than he actually was."

"How heavy was he?"

She thought a long moment. "Well..."

"What?"

"He looked obese at first, possibly eighty or a hundred pounds overweight. He wore sweats or jackets every time he came, so I can't be sure, but he seemed peculiarly soft. I had the feeling all of his bulk wasn't fat...exactly. He didn't seem to be at all sensitive when we had physical contact, like when he bumped into me. I think he wore padding under his clothes, maybe it was for camouflage, to give the illusion of being heavier than he was."

Marsh puzzled. "How about his hands?"

"They were large, but not pudgy. He wore latex gloves, the throwaway kind. I told you that. Remember?" They walked in silence until she pointed and said, "It's right over there."

Marsh whipped around to look where she pointed, then glanced back at her, confused.

"The municipal pool," she said. "You said you wanted to see the swimming pool. There it is."

He exhaled, trying to keep a lid on his volatile emotions as he turned to study the landmark. He had forgotten. He had asked her to take him there as a distraction, something to allay the tension between them. The ploy was no longer necessary. "Yeah. That's nice. Very nice."

"It looks better in the summer, with water in it."

"I'm sure it does." He continued pacing, following a path which wound over a grassy knoll. She looked around another moment, then hurried to catch up and swung back into step beside him. He smiled down at her, pleased by her effort. Obviously she, too, felt comfortable strolling together.

She returned the smile, her expression puzzled. He needed to get their conversation back on track before she read something in his face he wasn't ready for her to see and was making a heroic effort to hide.

"We were talking about your kidnapper. What else did you notice about him? Anything else unusual? Anything that sets him apart from other people."

She regarded a length of privet hedge. His eyes followed hers before he realized she was not seeing the bushes but was thinking.

"What is it?"

She shook her head and walked to a picnic table, stepped onto the bench, pivoted and sat on the table, gazing back toward the empty pool.

"The only other remarkable thing about him was the way he smelled. He had a yeasty odor."

Marsh nodded. "I read that in the police report. Yeast? The kind you cook with?"

"Yes...or...I thought maybe he worked at the brewery over on the west side, or in a bakery, somewhere where he handled or was around yeast."

"That's probably a good guess. I don't think the police followed up on that."

"Also, I got the impression that his hands were calloused."

"I thought he wore gloves."

"He did, but his hands felt rough. Maybe he works in construction or does yard work, some kind of manual labor that toughened his hands like that.

"No one acted like either the smell or the rough hands were important, but I thought knowing about them might help find him. The policeman didn't seem interested in things I thought were unusual about him."

Marsh shook his head. He had new grist, new leads the police hadn't pursued. Actually, he had several new ideas.

Someone might have noticed a guy lugging an old mattress around the campus or buying women's pads and bikini panties in a drug store or shop near the performing arts center.

And the yeast smell and the rough hands.

Marsh scooped some acorns off the picnic table and chunked them one at a time at a line of ants winding its way up the side of a trash can ten feet away. He didn't want to look at Anna. He didn't want her to see his face or to guess how important her next answers were to him personally. "Did he leave you alone after that?"

She snorted a caustic laugh. "For a while. Then he came back."

"How long was he gone?"

"I have no idea. There was no way for me to judge the passing of time. After he'd been gone a while, I dozed, off and on."

"Okay, when he came back, what happened?"

"He didn't say anything and didn't come inside the cage. He just tossed a box of tampons through the bars.

"After he'd gone, I used the stuff, then I lay down and tucked the quilt all around me and tried to stay warm. The air was cool and I didn't want to start cramping. I get stomach cramps when I'm cold...you know, when I'm having a period.

"I wanted to conserve my energy and think, come up with a plan for getting out of there. I tried to get myself psyched to do battle."

Marsh frowned at her. "Didn't you know the police would be looking for you, that all you had to do was stall him until they got there?"

"I figured they were looking, but I didn't know how long it might take them to find me, and I didn't know how patient this guy might be, you know, with my period and all. It seemed obvious he'd taken my clothes for a reason and I couldn't think of any reason he might have for doing that that I was going to like.

"It was when I was resting, gearing up for the fight that I became aware I had an ally. I could feel someone strong sending me mental messages. I guess that was you."

She climbed down from the table, using the bench as a step, stood stiffly and stretched from side to side at the waist, then flexed her neck.

"Do you have a headache?" he asked.

"A little one. I've got aspirin in my purse, in the car."

"Are you ready to go?"

Her eyes locked with his. "If you are."

He smiled and shook his head. "No, I'm fine doing just what we're doing. Tell me more about our mental linkup, the way it was from your end."

Breaking their eye contact, she sat down on the bench and concentrated on pushing at her cuticles.

"At first I thought it was my imagination. I was one of those kids who had an imaginary playmate when I was little. I figured it was something like that—someone I imagined. But I decided it couldn't hurt to feel like a friendly was there. I was still on the edge, but it was like I wasn't facing things completely on my own anymore. There was someone backing me." She shot him a smile.

Trying to look more pleasant than he felt, Joe nodded and gave her the most sincere grin he could manage. It was feeble. He wanted to move on with this. "Did he come back?"

"Yes, he did. By then I had decided the best thing to do was to play along, try to appease him, lull him, make him confident so he'd get careless. I figured the period thing would buy me some time. He'd be too disgusted to bother me while that was going on.

"Also, I figured his confidence was pretty high already. He probably thought I was some featherbrained coed that he'd already outsmarted several times. I guessed he thought I was one of the contestants, before the glamour treatment.

"Anyway, the next time I heard him coming, I wrapped the quilt around me and stood up.

"Before he opened the door, he said, 'Put your hands in the cuffs.' I hitched the quilt tightly under my arms and knelt. I leaned a little to do what he said, but I only closed the handcuffs to the first notch. They were loose, so I could slip my hands out, jump up and run.

"The first thing he did was to put his foot in the middle of my back and shove me from a kneeling position onto my hands and knees. He reached down and pinched the cuffs so tight they dug into my flesh. Then he put his foot on my backside and pushed. I tried to keep my knees under me, but he stepped down hard forcing me to stretch flat on my stomach."

Anna suddenly stood and began walking back the way they had come. "The sun feels good. I like hearing the leaves crunch when we walk." She breathed deeply. "Marsh, I've told you more than I've told anyone else. Could we please not talk about it anymore?"

He stepped quickly to catch up as she cut across the grass, obviously aimed toward the parking area.

"Do you remember your first dance?" His question was innocuous, and he saw that it had the desired effect. Some of the tension seem to ease from her shoulders.

She turned and smiled at him ruefully as she slowed her pace. "When do you mean?"

"Your very first dance. How old were you?"

Her smile broadened. It appeared to be a pleasant memory. "Seventh grade. A sock-hop after a junior high football game."

"Who did you like?"

"What boy? Probably Barry Ginsberg."

"What did Barry Ginsberg look like?"

She might have blushed, but Marsh couldn't be sure since her heightened color could be from the walk or the warmth of the sunshine.

"Barry was tall, sturdier than most of the boys our age. He had longish dark hair and a big nose and..."

"And what?"

She giggled under her breath. "Slash dimples and big lips. It doesn't sound like it from that description, but he was very handsome." She laughed again and glanced at him coquettishly. "The truth is, he looked a little bit like you."

Marsh tried to quell the pride and the goofy grin the comparison inspired. "And did Barry ask you to dance?"

"Only to fast dance. Barry didn't ask me to slow dance until the ninth grade."

"That long, huh? And you still liked him?"

"No. But by then I liked him again."

"How did that feel, slow dancing with a guy you liked back then?"

She laughed lightly and rolled her eyes. "Like I was coming down with the flu or something. I got feverish. Nervous."

"Puppy love. I recognize the symptoms."

"I guess. Anyway, he charged into this mob of girls, which probably took some nerve, and asked me to dance. When I said okay, he took my hand and led me onto the gym floor."

"Another sock hop?"

"On the gymnasium floor? Of course."

"Did he take your hand like this?" He wrapped his hand around hers and she nodded, smiling as if she were drifting back in time. "And he led you onto the dance floor like this?" Another nod. "Then what?"

"Then he put both arms around my waist."

"Like this?"

Anna looked puzzled and shivered slightly, but allowed Joe to ease his arms around her in a non threatening move, without bringing their bodies into contact. She hummed muffled agreement that what he did was correct.

"And after a while did he get up enough nerve to put his cheek against yours?"

"Un-huh."

"Like this?"

"Yes. Only his face wasn't scratchy."

"Sorry about that." He held her gently, his chin against her temple, until he felt her relax. "And after a while, did he touch those big lips of his to the side of your face, like this?" He turned his face slightly and dipped his head to brush his lips against her soft, freckled cheek.

She gulped a breath.

Marsh tried to disregard the feel of her breasts swelling against his chest as she inhaled. He expected her to break away any minute, but she surprised him.

"He put both his hands on my back," she said, "just above my waist." She squirmed closer and Joe's arms tightened involuntarily.

"Like this?" He pressed her to him as his lips nuzzled down her ear. She trembled and he wondered if he was pushing her too far. Suddenly her hands, which had been resting on his biceps, slid higher and she wrapped both arms around his neck, pulling the length of her body against the length of his before she shivered again.

He liked what was happening, or what seemed to be happening, to both of them. Her responses were spontaneous, probably as innocent as they had been when she was fourteen or fifteen. He shuffled his feet and hummed, pretending to dance, trying to maintain the illusion.

"And after a while, did Barry finally get up the courage to kiss you?"

She recoiled slightly, but not enough to separate their bodies as Joe's mouth drifted and captured hers. She relaxed into the innocent little kiss, humming her agreement, making her lips vibrate beneath his.

It was Anna who attempted to deepen the kiss, but Joe drew back, ever so subtly. He was making huge, unexpected inroads into Anna's touch-me-not fortress. He didn't want to send her scampering back into her shell. He was holding his emotions in check but things were getting tenuous. His body was like a racehorse, threatening to take the bit in its teeth and go for the finish line.

He smiled into her face and loosened his arms, propping his hands at either side of her waist. Keeping her arms around his neck, she rocked her head back and opened her eyes dreamily.

"Nice," he crooned. "Very nice."

She blinked several times before her gaze lost its dreamy cast. She stiffened and focused an accusing glare on his face, pulling her arms from around his neck. He allowed her to put several paces between them. Obviously, she was surprised by her own behavior. Yes, he would call what they were doing progress. And that wasn't all he would call it.

With minimal conversation, they walked back to the car. Joe didn't attempt to hold her door for her. He didn't trust himself to get that close. He was consumed with agonizing thoughts of how the perp must have felt, having this woman in a cage, naked, all to himself. Just imagining himself in the guy's shoes aroused more than anger in Joe.

Settled in the driver's seat, he toyed with the car keys but didn't put them in the ignition. She seemed relaxed again and while he hated to interrupt her euphoria, pursuit of his goal was the reason he'd lulled her with the innocent little trip down memory lane, so she could continue with her account of the kidnapping. She was primed. It was time.

"So, what happened next in the cage?"

His question, in a hushed tone, seemed to annoy her. Her expression darkened. "I don't want to talk about that any more. I've already told you more than I told my own mother."

"Anna, you said it yourself. The sun feels good. It's a bright, beautiful, leaf-crunching day. You're comfortable with me. We're good together. There is never going to be a better time or place to bring it out in the open."

He lowered his voice to a coaxing tone. "Tell me what happened next. You were lying on your stomach, your hands in the cuffs and he was beside you. Take it from there."

She wagged her head from side to side looking pained.

A squirrel darted up an oak tree, his playmate in hot pursuit. Joe followed Anna's gaze to watch the pair spiral higher and higher into the branches, race onto a limb and out a flimsy twig. The leader leaped and sailed through the air. Just as it looked as if he might plummet, he caught a skinny limb on the next tree, righted himself, scrambled up to a joint and turned, heckling, all but daring his companion to follow.

Anna laughed quietly. "Dodged the bullet that time." She sobered. She didn't look at Marsh. "He yanked the quilt off of me."

Marsh cringed at the mental picture of her lying on her stomach, her hands locked in the cuffs over her head.

God, he hated the pervert for looking at her at that moment. He wanted to kill the bastard. He *was* going to kill him. That thought consoled him. Ideally, he'd kill the pervert with his bare hands. And he was going to do it in front of Anna. Give her closure. Then her nightmares of the whole episode would be over, for good. He smiled. For the first time in his life, the idea of doing murder comforted him.

There was a long silence. Finally, Anna spoke again. "He didn't say anything. It was partially dark in there but I supposed he could see me. I kept my eyes shut. I heard him moving around. From the sounds, I knew he was refilling the plastic water jug and changing the kitty litter in the latrine. Yuck. What a gruesome job. He did it without saying a word or making a sound.

"I just lay there, afraid to move or even to look. Eventually, he came over close to me and I braced myself, waiting. I didn't know if he would hit me or kick me or..." She choked. "Or touch me. He just stood there a long time, looking, I guess. Then he unlocked the cuffs and left."

"And what did you do?"

"I grabbed the quilt and rolled into a ball on the mattress and bawled.

"After that, I moved the mattress into the other dark corner, away from the latrine, but even there, it was touching the pole with the handcuffs on it. The room was too small to get the mattress away from the pole."

"What were you thinking, then?"

"I was in a panic, hardly able to think at all. I felt helpless...and hopeless. Eventually, listening to the hum of the machine in the distance, I kind of pulled myself together. And I caught more vibes from my secret source."

She suddenly looked intently at Joe and choked again as her voice managed to whisper, "Thank you for being there then. Thank you for that from the bottom of my heart."

He nodded and waited, his temper sizzling so it seared a headache, which made him wonder idly about Anna's headache, the one she'd mentioned earlier. He didn't want to ask, to risk interrupting her, now that she was talking freely again.

"I leached encouragement from my imaginary friend," she continued. "I realize now, of course, that that energy, that strength probably was coming from you." She frowned and he grimaced.

"I guess," he said.

"But, of course, then I didn't know it was you."

"How long before the guy came back?"

"I told you, I had no way to measure time. No way to tell day from night or anything." She looked surprised. "What time is it now, anyway?"

He glanced at her wrist. "Don't you have a watch?"

"I have a couple but I don't like to wear them. There are always clocks around. The one in the company car works fine."

"Why do you care what time it is now?"

"I'm hungry."

He grinned. "Okay, let's eat." He inserted the key and started the engine. The digital clock on the dash read 3:35. "What do you feel like eating?"

"How about chicken enchiladas? We've got the ingredients and the recipe."

"Can you wait that long?"

"Yes. I'll make a salad. We can munch on veggies or chips while you're cooking."

"Can we make the butterscotch brownies too?"

She grinned. "What do you mean 'we?'" He laughed at her insight as she continued. "That big ego of yours is not quite so confident of it's performance in the kitchen, is it?"

He grimaced, pretending to be one-upped. "Let's say I have more expertise in other rooms."

"Dozing in easy chairs in the living room?" She smirked.

He arched his eyebrows, conveying a subtle warning. "Be careful or I might tell you where I *draw* the rave reviews."

"Let me guess. The *drawing room*."

He chuckled. "Ah, you're a closet punster, I see."

Her smile dissolved to a disapproving glower which he hoped was not due to her recollected image of the bare-bottomed waitress darting into the hallway at Wesley's apartment. That was when Stemmons first warned her about Joe's punning. He didn't want her conjuring up any ugly pictures.

Joe's mental processes led him from up to down again. He couldn't seem to shake the image of Anna lying cuffed, face down, nude except for the necessary bikini panties. Again, images of her ordeal aroused more in him than simple indignation and he was angry with himself for his impure urgings.

Chapter Thirteen

At her apartment, Joe retrieved the newspaper on Anna's porch, scanned her story about the fire, and complimented it and Wesley's pictures. "You and Lee are a good team."

"I'm good with anybody. Ask around." She laughed self consciously, obviously suddenly aware of the innuendo.

He slanted her a suggestive look. "Really? Well, step right this way." He waved his hand toward her bedroom.

She sobered. "That's not funny, Marsh."

"I didn't mean it to be." He lost the smile. "I like you, Anna Fulenweider. I like you even more than I expected to, which is saying a lot." He waited until her eyes met his before he dropped his voice and continued. "And you like me too. I can tell." He sidled her direction and was surprised that she stayed riveted where she stood.

"Now, when a man and a woman enjoy a mutual attraction, it's normal for them to want to spend time together and, eventually, for them to touch each other, casually, and even kiss each other, when the spirit moves them." He offered a hand.

She started to reach for it, then frowned into his face and shook her head. "No."

He waited until she had gone into the kitchen, her back to him over the bar, before he grinned. She was coming around. It was slow, but she was moving in the right direction. She had already been in his arms—twice. He had even kissed her. He needed to be patient. God help him.

Anna was relaxed, tearing fresh spinach into a bowl while Joe placed pieces of cooked chicken over broken tortilla shells in a casserole dish before he returned to the hated subject.

"What happened the next time this pervert came to your cage?"

"Do we have to talk about that now?"

"Yes. We're here in your well-lighted kitchen, both of us with our hands occupied. There couldn't be a better time."

"That's what you said at the park."

"It was true then too."

"Marsh, can't we skip it, just for tonight?"

"No." He settled a firm scowl on her pleading eyes, but didn't dare speak, knowing he might fold because of the way her lips formed that delectable pout. Her mouth often reflected her moods, smiling when she approved things, her lips pursed when she was displeased. He wondered if the occasional pout had gotten the desired results when she was a child. He would bet money it had.

"It gets pretty sick," she said, bringing him back to the present problem.

"Just tell it straight out like it's some repulsive news story you covered."

She took a breath and directed her full attention to the spinach. "Before he came in, he told me to lock my hands in the cuffs. I wrapped the quilt around me and secured the edges as well as I could before I did what he said. I didn't make the cuffs too loose or too tight. He told me to get on my hands and knees. The quilt was still over me, but it swung loose, hanging down on the sides.

"The first thing he did, of course, was yank the quilt off. I didn't look at him. I didn't want to see him looking at me. I couldn't have seen him very well, even if I had looked. It was darker, like it was nighttime or maybe the weather was bad. I couldn't tell."

She paused to get fresh mushrooms, green onions, a tomato, and feta cheese from the refrigerator, juggling them. With both hands and her forearms occupied, she pushed the refrigerator door closed with a foot.

When she began chopping the vegetables with singular dedication, Marsh figured she didn't plan to continue her narrative. "And?"

She looked at him, her expression again pleading. "You won't understand about the next part, Marsh."

"Try me."

"I didn't have any choice." Her voice faded to a sigh. "I haven't told anyone because I can't figure out how to convince them that I didn't encourage him." She shot him a pleading look and he nodded. "I didn't want to...to encourage him, that is. I didn't try to. Honestly, I didn't."

"Okay, Anna, anyone with any sense *knows* this situation wasn't your doing. We all know you weren't the one calling the shots." His voice operated on its own, the volume rising until he practically shouted. "Tell me what happened, damn it."

He didn't want to sound like that, be either impatient or angry, but she wasn't the only one feeling the strain.

She stared at the salad ingredients, but didn't move. "I was on my hands and knees, you understand."

He nodded impatiently. He had the picture.

"He got down on the floor beside the mattress."

Marsh froze, barely able to hear her over the sound of the water running on the vegetables she was fooling with in the sink. He wanted to tell her to turn it off but he didn't want to interrupt her again.

"He rolled onto his back and sort of slid his face underneath me." Her eyes shot to his, obviously wanting to evaluate the effect her story had on his opinion of her.

He forced himself to remain stoic, not moving, not displaying any emotion at all. She turned off the water and the room seemed to hang in a chill, deathly silence.

"The way he did it...well, it was the way a mechanic slides under a car, only it was just his head." She paused.

"Did he touch you?"

She shook her head no, biting her lips.

"What *did* he do?"

"Nothing. He just lay there breathing, looking at my bare breasts hanging over his face." She glowered at Marsh, her mouth set in a grim line. "I arched my back as much as I could to keep from touching him. But there was nothing else I could do, no way to get away from him. It was terrible. Sweat ran down my neck and trickled under my armpits. It felt like bugs crawling. It made me crazy.

"Finally, when I couldn't stand it any longer and thinking I needed to do something to break that evil spell, I asked him what time it was.

"He didn't answer.

"I asked what day it was.

"He wouldn't talk. I could feel him breathing, his breathe hot against my flesh under there, but he didn't touch me and he didn't say a word.

"That's the first time I got the shakes—you know, the bad ones, like I get now?" Tears seeped down her flushed cheeks and Marsh realized she probably couldn't see the green onion she was chopping. Was the onion causing the tears? He didn't think so.

"I couldn't help it, don't you see?" She had begun babbling, sobbing and talking at the same time as she swiped at her eyes with the back of her wrist. Her voice cracked. "I tried to get control of my body, or my voice, but I was shaking so bad, I couldn't think."

Slowly she turned from the sink and blinked at Marsh, as if she were trying to clear her vision. She was trembling all over. He reached for her, but she shook her head and looked as if she might bolt. He withdrew the hand and waited.

"I asked him to let me go, Marsh. I didn't want to beg. I didn't want to sound as desperate as I felt. I tried to appeal to his sense of honor or decency." She was thoughtful for a long moment. "I'm not sure, but I don't believe he has either one.

"That's when I remembered you, Marsh, my imaginary friend inside my head. It made me stronger, so strong that I tried threatening him."

Marsh gave her a tight smile of encouragement.

"I said people would be looking for me, that they'd come, that they'd find me, that I could feel them getting closer every minute."

"Had he moved or was he still underneath you? What did he say?"

As she turned back to the sink, the paring knife clattered into the basin and she caught herself, bracing both hands on the countertop. Marsh took a step forward before she flapped a hand, waving him off.

"I didn't really believe him, Marsh. I knew he wasn't telling me the truth, but somehow, there with him, with no one else..."

Marsh felt like a statue, poised mid step in the middle of her kitchen, waiting.

"He said no one was looking for me. No one was coming." Her voice dropped to a whisper. "He said no one even knew I was gone."

Marsh felt the crushing mental effect of her tormentor's words and he seethed.

It wasn't enough that the perp had stolen her body, he was also playing with her head. Marsh's resolve deepened. He *was* going to murder this guy, and he was going to do it slowly, strip him, humiliate him, torture him, torment him, exactly the way the guy had tormented her.

She inhaled. "I called him a liar. I shouted it at him and the words sounded strong, but what he'd said had knocked me for a loop, the idea that no one was looking for me. Intellectually I was nearly sure he was lying, but he had planted a seed of doubt and I couldn't seem to get it out of my head."

Anna's eyes shot to Joe's face. "Oh, how I hung onto you then. I needed you, whether you were imaginary or not, and I reached out to you with everything I had."

She picked up a handful of mushrooms, then dropped them, and turned around quickly, wiping her hands on her dress.

Directly in front of her, facing her, Marsh kept his arms at his sides. "I'm here now, Anna, just as surely as I was there then, holding you, keeping you afloat, treading water. You know that. You felt our closeness then. You feel it now. Don't you?"

He didn't move as her trembling hand reached up and cool, damp fingers touched his jaw. Then she lowered her hands to her sides, moved a step forward and bumped her forehead against his chest again and again.

"When he was there, under me, he breathed harder and harder until he was all but panting, wheezing, with his mouth wide open." She cleared her throat. "I froze, afraid if I moved, afraid I might accidentally touch him and precipitate...something. I was terrified, shaking so bad I thought I'd pass out.

"Then he slithered out from under me. He stood up and tossed the quilt over me and unlocked the cuffs."

"Did you think he might be impotent?"

"I didn't know what to think, except that his behavior seemed strange. But I was too relieved, too thankful that looking at me was all he did."

She backed away from Marsh, turned and picked up three of the mushrooms scattered in the sink.

Joe said, "Tell me your impression of his size then. Describe his face."

She gave a caustic little laugh. "He had a painted face, had made himself a weird mask, like one of those harlequin things. When he spoke, it seemed obvious he was disguising his voice. It was something more than just the whisper."

"Did the mask frighten you?"

She looked through him, apparently considering the question. "Actually, it had the opposite effect. Again when I thought about it, I realized the disguise reinforced the idea that he planned to let me go, eventually. What I didn't know was when. I wondered if I could prod him, make him want to let me go sooner than later.

"The next time I heard him coming, I was not as afraid since it didn't look like he planned to rape me. I took courage from that.

"But the room was lighter when he came the next time. His skin looked chalky. He ran through the same routine, made me put on the cuffs and get on my hands and knees before he came into the cage. Then he ripped off the quilt, like it was part of some ritual. I still thought he was detestable, but the routine was more familiar, less threatening.

"He slithered under me. I arched my back again, raising myself as far away from him as I could to make sure I didn't accidentally touch him.

"Like before, he lay there a long time and the only sound was his breathing as it got heavier and faster. My back ached from holding it arched and my arms started to tremble. Apparently he had been waiting for a sign I was weakening because that's when he touched me." She sobbed, a small, mewling sound. "He put one hand on my breast."

Bracing both hands, she leaned on the sink. Marsh turned off the burner under a stick of margarine melting in a saucepan, then moved closer to put an arm around her waist. She struggled halfheartedly as he guided her into the living area.

"Sit." His voice was graveled, a growl which sounded as if he would brook no argument.

Anna sank onto the sofa, covered her face with her hands and rocked back and forth over her knees.

If her kidnapper were in that room at that moment, Marsh knew he could grab the S.O.B. with his bare hands, would enjoy the sound of neck bones splintering as he twisted the man's head off. Marsh had never considered himself capable of that kind of violence, but this perp had taken him to a whole new level of outrage.

It might be better if he didn't hear any more.

Yet, in spite of her present broken condition, Anna appeared to be getting stronger as she expelled her story.

He shouldn't be hearing this. But he was the one who had her confidence—the only one she'd been willing to confide in. This was one damned untenable situation.

She didn't cry, as he'd expected, but breathed deeply once, twice, and again. When she finally looked at him, her face was marked by ashen defiance. Suddenly, her face twisted, her fist shot up, the middle finger stiff, and she shook it at the door.

Her giggle sounded maniacal at first, before it became harsh, determined laughter. When she quieted, she said, "I'm going to have to see him again, aren't I, Marsh? You and I are going to track him down, aren't we? We're going to get him. Isn't that right?"

Marsh bobbed his head up and down several times, a silent, determined assent.

"And you'll hold him for me, and let me take first crack at him, won't you?"

Joe shrugged and tried not to rejoice in her wicked grin. "Yeah, Anna, I'm afraid if that's what you want when the time comes, that's exactly what's going to happen. Heaven help the poor bastard if he falls into our clutches first. This guy is going to need serious police protection. I don't know if he'd be safe from us even if he got into the federal witness protection program."

She laughed out loud. "He'd better have a darn good imaginary friend when I get my hands on him. That's all I know, because it's going to take a real tough guy to defeat my imaginary friend, isn't it, Marsh?"

Marsh couldn't muffle the rolling laugh which began in his chest and rumbled up to explode into the room. "Ain't anybody gonna stop you and me together, Fulenweider. You can bet the farm on that."

Chapter Fourteen

"So, after he tweaked your boob, what happened?"

Marsh sifted flour into a bowl of moist ingredients. Since she had finished the salad, Anna stood close beside him breaking pecans into a measuring cup for the brownie batter.

She grimaced and gave him a disbelieving look, then laughed, apparently at his terminology, just as he had planned for her to do.

"He didn't *tweak* my boob, Marsh. He molested me."

"Fondled you?"

"No. Molested me," she corrected.

"Did he molest you gently?"

"Well, yes, I guess so."

"Sensuously?"

She hesitated, blushed and stared at the pecans she was breaking. "Yes."

"And you would be something of an authority on a man's touching your breasts *sensuously*, is that right?"

She shot him a dark look, clenched her jaw, and broke pecans with new vigor. "It's happened."

"You sound like you might have enjoyed it."

The minute the words were out, he regretted them. If that were the reason she hadn't told anyone details, because she was afraid she'd be accused of enjoying the perp's behavior, he had knifed directly into her most vulnerable spot.

She narrowed her eyes, set her mouth, got out a cake pan, dipped her fingers in the shortening and began to apply it before she raised the hand lacquering the pan with shortening and gave him the bird, shaking her middle finger in his face with the same enthusiasm she'd shown making the same gesture toward the front door on two earlier occasions.

His usual smug smile waffled. He deserved that. He was quiet for a long moment before he repeated the question in a calm, coaxing tone. "Did you like it, Anna?"

She snapped her response. "Why would you even ask me something like that?"

"Okay." Something niggled hairs on the back of his neck. He'd struck a nerve. He would have to pursue that line again later. "What else did he do?"

"I don't know. I don't want to talk about it anymore."

"Come on. How long did he touch you? To what extent? Did he touch you below the waist? What?" He hated this more and more with every question he himself posed, conjuring mental pictures which were obviously unpleasant for her and which were making him crazy.

"In those same circumstances, Marsh, what would most men have done? They have a naked woman in their clutches, bound, disoriented, unable to defend herself. I suppose you'll say you would have done the honorable thing and released her, right?"

He felt the heat in his face as his fists tightened. He was disgusted by the familiar straining in his trousers at the thought of having Anna in that position and at his mercy.

"Get us some cuffs, come in the bedroom with me and we'll see what I'd do." He remained as he stood, focusing his frustration on beating the cookie batter.

"That's not happening, Marsh. I'd never voluntarily put myself in that position with you or any other man. Not in this lifetime."

He spoke quietly. "That very scenario may happen someday, Anna, but even I am not insensitive enough to think it's going to be today."

Joe set the whisk aside and eased around to stand behind her.

"What are you doing?" She jerked around, nearly putting her fist in his face.

"Waiting for you." He intentionally made the words sound suggestive.

Her rounded eyes searched his face, as if trying to see if he meant what she thought he meant and certain that he couldn't.

"The batter's ready," he said, clarifying.

She shifted her gaze to the bowl.

"You're sure taking your own sweet time busting up those pecans."

She glanced at the clock on the stove. "It's only four-thirty. We've got plenty of time. Wesley won't be here until five-fifteen at the earliest."

"Well, then, I'd say we do have plenty of time." Tentatively, he put his hands on her shoulders. She flinched, but didn't withdraw from his touch.

Bracing his hands, he used his thumbs to rub the base of her neck. The muscles above her shoulder blades were in knots. Silent moments passed before she rocked her head back, let her shoulders slump a little, and exhaled. She stood perfectly still, allowing him to work away the tension.

Moving carefully, he put one arm in front of her shoulders to brace them as he set the heel of his hand in the middle of her back to rub. Gradually, when he felt her relax, he worked his way down, shifting his hands to follow the outline of her ribs, to her waist, massaging her lower back with his thumbs.

He slipped both hands along her belt line from back to front and tugged, pulling the back of her snugly to the front of him. She struggled only halfheartedly when he gathered her full breasts in his hands. When she wriggled, he froze, steadying her.

"There, sweetheart," he crooned against her ear. "It's me. It's only me. You're okay. I just want to hold you a minute. I won't hurt you. I promise. Not ever. You're safe with me and you know it."

She stood there quietly, letting him knead her breasts for a long moment before she said lazily, "Quit."

"You're a woman who likes being fondled, aren't you, Anna? You like me putting my hands on you. You have some idea of how beautiful you are, don't you? You know how much I like holding these full, ripe melons of yours, don't you? You enjoy being worshiped, don't you, Anna? By men. By all men."

She huffed and shuffled out of his grasp, lowered her head and stared at her hands as she rubbed them together, dusting off the grit left by the pecans.

Marsh tried to get her to look at him. "Did he handle you gently, Anna? Did he worship you?"

Although he couldn't see her whole face, he could tell her frown deepened.

"Um," she answered affirmatively without looking at him.

"Do you feel guilty, Anna, that you are a passionate woman? That you respond to a man's hands when he's gentle with you? Are you ashamed of being flattered when your body makes a man hot? Twice you mentioned how hard he breathed when he looked at you. Do you like having the power, knowing that touching you sets a guy panting? You've told me that more than once about how hard the perp breathed when he was close to you. Did you feel like you were in control of things when you could light him up like that?"

Her words were so quiet, he almost didn't hear them. "I didn't *want* to like it."

Marsh tried to keep his response soft, too, making it more of a statement than a question. "But you did."

She bit both her upper and lower lips. Her head bowed, she walked all the way into the living room, to the couch and sank. "I was every bit as depraved as he was."

Marsh eased down next to her. After a long moment, she raised her eyes to his as if she were mortified to be having this conversation. "You're the only one...the only other person alive who knows...that...about...me. Please don't tell anyone. Please, Marsh...not anyone."

He snorted, part cough, part annoyance as he made super human effort not to wrap his arms around her. "Anna, don't you see how perfect, how wonderfully normal your physical reaction was?

"If you restrained me, touched me, stimulated me, no matter how much I didn't want it to, my body would respond, to the ultimate degree, if you pushed it." He almost smiled at the truth of that statement. "The only thing your physical responses show, Anna, is that you're a wholesome, healthy, red-blooded female. Pleasure is a valid response to sexual stimulation."

He held his hands out, palms up, encouraging her to touch him. Her eyes snapped with sudden anger. "How about shame?"

"You're ashamed that you like being touched? Honey, grown men and women are specifically engineered—

designed by their Maker—to react exactly as you did to that very thing.

"Hell, Anna, I get excited when I look at you and you blush; when I brush against you, and you tremble. My guess is your responsiveness blasted this poor slob into orbit."

"But I begged him to stop." She hesitated and looked even more forlorn. "And finally he did."

"He did?"

"I was so ashamed, I couldn't stand it. I cried like a baby. It seemed like as soon as he discovered I liked having his hands on me, he stopped. And he seemed to be happy about it, like he was pleased that he was able to torment me with my own weakness. He slid out from under me and rolled up onto his hands and knees and started humming." She paused.

"And what did you do?"

"Me? I quit bawling. I thought he was going to leave." She exhaled a tiny sob, then stammered. "By then, I...I didn't want him to. I wanted him to stay." She hesitated and her voice dropped to a whisper. "And I told him so."

Marsh nodded indicating he understood but didn't trust his voice to hide his disapproval. How could she have given in to the bastard like that? So easily? How could she give him an open invitation to help himself?

Dr. Ware's words echoed in his brain. *Don't judge what she tells you. Don't second guess her behavior.*

He was still chiding himself when she began to speak again. "I think he was trying to comfort me then because he patted my shoulder. But then he slid his hand across my back, over my hips, down my thighs, along my calves, all the way to my toes. He knelt down and grabbed my foot. He just hunkered there a minute, squeezing that one foot in both his hands."

"What did that mean?"

"I have no idea. Then he jumped up, keyed the cuffs and ran out of there like the very devil was after him."

Anna stood and paced the living area, wringing her hands. "I shouldn't have told you that...not the part about my personal thoughts."

"Why not?"

She shot him an accusing look. "Because neither of us has the training to understand what it means." She looked startled. "And because you liked me." She lowered her voice. "Because I liked you. And because now you know I'm a closet slut."

"I told you, Anna. There's no way you were or are or ever will be responsible for what happened. I want to know about every minute of the time you spent there. Everything you can recall. You still haven't told me all of it. I need to hear it all. But, baby, I don't need to hear it nearly as much as you need to tell it." He gave her a moment. "What did you do after he left that time?"

"I pulled the cover over me. Of course, except for the chill, it didn't seem to matter anymore if I was naked or not. He'd seen it all. I thought maybe he'd left because I disgusted him.

"Anyway, he was gone and I should have been relieved." She choked and coughed, as if she were stalling, delaying the next revelation. Finally, after several false starts she practically exploded, keeping her eyes lowered.

"I wanted him to come back, Marsh. I wanted him to stay with me." She squinted at Joe. "Realizing that I wanted him to stay there made me more ashamed of myself than I'd ever been before in my life.

"And I could feel you, my imaginary friend, encouraging me, helping, without having a clue about the wicked person I was," she gasped, "about what a whore I was turning out to be."

Marsh had a hard time following her line of thought through the emotional maze that took her to such an outrageous conclusion.

Where the hell was all the guilt coming from? He didn't want to interrupt and wasn't sure how to frame the questions anyway. He held silent while she composed herself, then she continued. "You don't understand. It's like he made me love him."

"Love him? You mean you made love to him?"

Her eyes sparked. "No!"

"What do you mean then, he made you love him? You *loved* him?"

She blinked several times and regarded him with a dark scowl. "Yes," but the word was more a question than confirmation. "You don't know how he made me feel. I actually wanted him to... I mean I've never wanted anyone like that before. I was never so ashamed in my life, still, at the same time, I wanted him to touch me. Obviously, I had fallen for him...and, at the same time, I hated him."

Her eyes were wide with fear and wonder.

Marsh shook his head, having gained sudden insight.

"No, Anna. He stimulated you. Sexually, he made your body want more of what he offered. But that wasn't love, sweetheart. You know that. What he aroused was your basic, garden variety lust. He was capitalizing on the physical desire God programmed into you, a physical need a man knows he can satisfy. But lust isn't love. Surely you know that by now, after hanging out with me."

Staring at him, Anna tilted her head slightly as if she were perplexed. He had her full attention, but obviously she wasn't clear about what he meant.

"How did you feel yesterday when you were working on your computer and you looked over to see me slack-jawed, crashed in your easy chair?"

She winced and bit back a grin. "Safe."

"And how did you feel when we were walking in the park, talking? Did you notice we were always in step?" She nodded sheepishly. "How did that make you feel?"

"I don't know...companionable."

"And when I was clowning around, rolling around like an idiot on the floor?"

She smiled. "That was funny."

"And you laughed until you cried."

"Yeah." Her smile, bright for a moment, dimmed, but he wasn't through.

"Remember how you felt at the fire when you thought the wall had fallen on me?"

"Terrified."

"You run all those emotional gambits, Anna, because you care about me. You and I are developing a genuine, mutual regard.

"Now, you may not realize this, sugar, but I can light you up, get you more excited sexually, of your own free will, than the pervert who had you locked up ever could. Do you want me show you? I can. Right here. Right now."

Before she could begin to object, he continued, lowering his voice. "Did you think about me when you got in bed last night, Anna? Did you dream about me, even before you fell asleep?"

He reached out to put his fingers on her elbows. "In the privacy of those moments, did you touch yourself intimately? Did you think about me touching you in those private places? Of touching me? Of kissing me? Of showering with me? Did you?"

She began shaking her head before he added, "Be honest, Anna. Be honest with both of us. Do you wonder how I know what you might have thought about in your bed last night?"

Her eyes rounded and he grinned.

"No, I didn't read your mind, baby. I know about those private thoughts, Anna, because I was lying in my bed entertaining those very same thoughts myself. I lay there in the cool night air thinking about you until I made myself sweat and squirm with wanting you so bad."

She shot a quick look at his face, maybe to see if he was kidding, then bit her lips and lowered her eyes to stare at her own hands which were tightly clasped in front of her. But she didn't make any attempt to escape either his words or his touch.

Then her thoughts drifted and returned to their earlier conversation. "I wondered how what I felt for the pervert could be love. If it was, I didn't want any part of it. But how else can you explain why I missed him when he was gone, if that wasn't love?"

He grinned. "Because he had to lock you up and make you his prisoner and frighten you half to death before you felt anything but disgust. Anyone could have explained that to you, if you had talked to someone about it."

She stared at him. "I didn't want anyone else to know. I cried and cried and worried myself sick afraid other people would find out about me, until I realized he couldn't very well tell anyone else how I behaved without implicating himself.

"All I had to do was get out of there alive. He was the only person who would ever have to know this awful, sickening weakness in me, that I could fall for such a sick-o. I figured likes attract. So I promised myself I'd never tell another living soul."

She looked at Marsh as if seeing him for the first time. "I guess, well, spilling my guts like this to you, I'm going to have to kill you now to insure your silence."

He laughed lightly as she grimaced and risked a quick glance at him. She shuddered, looked as if she were fighting a painfully teary grin, and hiccupped. Marsh studied her watery smile, but didn't speak. A long silence ensued before he thought her calm enough for them to continue.

Deciding it was all right to prod her again, he said, "When he came back, what happened?"

"Lord," she wailed, leaped to her feet, and stormed toward the kitchen, not turning until she stood in the doorway. "Haven't you had enough? I know I have. I've told you too much already. I'm through. No more. Confession's over. If I don't perpetuate that awful experience, no one else can. No one else knows. My truest prayer is that I can forget it. Maybe someday, when that happens, maybe I'll be able to understand, maybe even forgive myself." She cast him a sharp look. "But now that's only if you don't blab."

She walked on into the kitchen. Marsh took a dozen quick steps and grabbed her hand. She jerked away as if he'd scalded her and darted to the sink where she grabbed the paring knife and whirled, pointing the business end of it at his stomach.

Moving slowly, Marsh reached around her and turned on the water. He kept his tone level as he said, "I have to wash my hands and finish making the brownies."

The plug covered the drain and water collected in the basin. Anna withdrew the point of the knife, which hovered inches from his gut, spun, and stared at the pooling water. Her breathing became labored and she began to tremble.

"What is it, Anna? Is it the water?"

She shook her head.

"What does water have to do with the cage?"

She bit her lips and continued shaking her head.

"Drinking water? No? Water for washing then? Is that what you're remembering?"

Her eyes shot to his face and the palsied shakes which had been absent all day took her with a renewed vengeance.

The knife slipped out of her hand and clattered on the hardwood floor between their feet.

Her knees knocked as she sank into a heap, quaking and babbling. Joe knelt beside her, resisting the urge to put his arms around her, clenching his teeth, and balling his hands into impotent fists, waiting for the shaking to subside.

Startled by several sharp raps on the outside door, he looked up as Wesley swooped into the condo with no other fanfare. The newcomer assessed the situation in a heartbeat.

"Marsh," Stemmons roared, "what in hell are you doing to her?"

Wesley's long legs swallowed the living area in half-a-dozen strides and he dropped onto the kitchen floor beside Anna, elbowing his way in, cutting between her and Joe.

"Hey, baby. It's okay. I'm here. Everything's all right. No one's gonna touch you 'cept me." He glared at Marsh. Wesley's look drove the out-of-town visitor back.

Stemmons cooed gentling words, quieted her gradually without touching her. Finally, he offered a hand to help her up. She reached out to him, accepting assistance, and Marsh marveled, wondering if or when Stemmons would notice how far she had come in only a day.

Conversation at dinner was stilted. Wesley asked both Anna and Joe several times what they'd done all afternoon. They told him about the walk in the park and supper preparations, but neither of them made any reference to the main theme of their conversations.

They were all three kicked back on the sofa facing the television when the nightly news commentator did a voice over on commotion on the university's fraternity row.

The Phi Eps were hosting their annual dog and pony show.

Fraternity brothers made a list of "The Homeliest Girls on Campus," a list actually composed of attractive girls who had dumped members of that fraternity in the past year. The object was to taunt the nominees into participating in the games.

To race, the guys crawled over the grassy area on their hands and knees. Joe glanced at Anna, who's face had blanched. "What are they doing?" she asked in a whisper.

Without noticing the change in Anna's voice, Wesley explained. "Watch this. It's hilarious. The guys pretend to be the ponies and the girls are the dogs who get on their backs, and they race."

Anna's groan, muffled into her cupped hands, could have been mistaken for a yawn, except that she suddenly lurched to her feet and darted into her bedroom. Marsh was right behind her. She threw herself across her bed diagonally on her stomach and sobbed into her pillow. He sat on the bed beside her.

"What did you see, Anna? Did you recognize someone? What is it?"

"I'd give anything...if you didn't...have to be...the one." She blubbered and it took him a moment to understand the words. Even then the meaning eluded him.

"Easy, tiger. I'm here to help. Tell me what's wrong."

Wesley pushed the door wide, staring at the two together on the bed. His disapproval was apparent, but Marsh had other concerns and waved Stemmons back. The man studied the situation a long moment before he retreated to the living room, leaving the door ajar.

"Okay, now what is it?" Joe tried to keep his voice steady, but the annoyance was there, in his words. He thought about the pictures they'd just seen, the students cavorting on their hands and knees... Then he got an inkling.

"Did he mount you, Anna? The kids playing around like that, did it remind you of something that happened?"

He bowed his head and covered his face with one hand. Then, knowing it was wrong, he gave into the angst. "Why, Anna? Why did you let him do that? Did he force you? Tell me he doped you or hurt you to make you let him do that to you."

But Anna continued sobbing into her pillow without saying a word.

Chapter Fifteen

Anna fidgeted and ground her teeth in her sleep.

Slouched in the bedside chair, Marsh straightened and blinked himself awake. He didn't know how she could sleep that way, with all the damned lights blazing.

Although she was perspiring, Anna clutched the covers to her chin. Occasionally she thrashed around. To add to the problem, she insisted on sleeping fully clothed. He didn't know if that was her habit since her ordeal, or if she was just deferring to his presence.

It had been a battle, convincing Stemmons to leave them alone for the night, but Anna had finally chimed in and won him over.

She groaned, flinching again.

"What is it, Anna?" Marsh kept his voice low. "What's happening there in your head? In your dreams?"

Her eyes opened to slits and she frowned at him, looking startled for a moment before she came more fully awake.

"Tell me what's going on," he pressed quietly. "Is he there, in your head?"

"Yes." She attempted a phony laugh.

"Were you in the cuffs?"

She nodded and looked annoyed.

"On your hands and knees?"

"He made me let him, Marsh. I didn't want it."

"Okay." He'd beaten himself up all night about what he'd said. He'd condemned her bitterly, words spewing from his own anger. It was exactly what Ware had warned him *not* to do. He had to make it up to her. "Did he bring something with him? A prop of some kind?"

"A bucket of water and...and a bath sponge."

"Okay." Marsh wanted to proceed slowly. "He told you to put on the cuffs, as usual, is that right?"

She turned her face away from him, but nodded.

"He opened the cage and came in?"

Closing her eyes, she groaned, rolled onto her side with her back to him, and pulled her knees to her chest.

"Did you see him set the bucket down?"

"Yes." Her voice was muffled.

"Then what?"

He thought she hadn't heard or had fallen back asleep by the time she finally said, "He yanked off the quilt. I knew he'd do that. He always did that. Always the same...like it was some big, dramatic moment, like he had an audience." She swallowed a sob which made a gurgling sound in her throat.

Marsh allowed her a minute. Finally she said, "He checked the cuffs to make sure I had done them tight enough, then he spread a towel on the floor by the mattress and nudged me with his knee until I shifted onto it." Another muffled sob.

Joe waited a dozen heartbeats. "And what did he do then?"

"He knelt beside me and pulled the panties down my legs and off. He hauled the sponge out of the water and slopped it over my backside. The water was warm and it felt good at first, until it started running everywhere. And then..." She paused again.

"Go on."

"He rubbed around my bottom and...between my legs." She choked a little but she wasn't crying. "And he touched me, you know...in the private places. I tried hard not to move, but Lord help me, I did."

It wasn't his desire to be patient that prevented Marsh from rushing her. It was the mental image. But he was beginning to get just a glimmer of a thought. Something that had happened between Anna and him that afternoon had planted the idea; a way to counter the dastardly deeds perpetrated by this pervert.

The plan incubating in his thoughts might not be approved by any practicing shrink, but then, no certified shrink had been able to get her to open up this way. He probably should keep going with his instincts. They seemed to be working pretty well so far.

She was whispering, hissing, chastising herself. He didn't want to let her to go too far with it.

"Okay, so he touched you. Men touch women. We do that, just about every chance we get. We love touching you.

Touching women is probably a boy's most primal urge from the time his eyes open at birth. That, and eating. It's really not that big a surprise that this pervert should want to touch you intimately. And he might have wanted to see if he could get a rise out of you."

Her eyes popped open and glittered with a sudden, consuming malice. Marsh tried a withering smile which had no effect.

"He rubbed the inside of his forearm back and forth between my legs." She turned her face into the pillow. "It was the worst moment of my life." She paused for several seconds, then glowered at him and said, "I got so turned on, I could hardly breathe."

Joe straightened in his chair and returned the glower, which seemed to encourage her.

"He put his chest against my side. He reached under me with the other hand and massaged my breasts. He got his hand sudsy and when my skin was slick, he rubbed me, all over. He pretended he was washing me, but that's not what he was doing and we both knew it."

Turning, wild-eyed, she yanked the sheet over her head and moaned but the pitiful wail got louder until it was a banshee scream.

Marsh endured as long as he could before he moved to the edge of her bed. He grabbed the sheet where her hands were and caught her wrists in a grip tight enough to silence her. He didn't pull the sheet away from her face, but allowed her to remain hidden.

She seethed, swinging her head from side to side. "I hated myself then, for feeling how I felt. I hate myself for it now."

"Anna, those were perfectly natural responses to someone touching you in places created to be sensitive. That bastard knew it. He knew the kind of response he'd get. Don't you realize he knew that?"

"But why did he want it?"

"Maybe to see if he could. Maybe he guessed you didn't know how erotic your own responses might be." A sudden, compelling thought sneaked into Marsh's mind and he spoke again, thinking out loud. "Maybe it's someone you know; someone you've rejected; someone who knows you and realizes that, as smart as you are, you still are not real astute about things sexual."

She groaned, still hidden beneath the sheet. "No, no, no. It's *not* someone I know." Her voice dropped. "It can't be. I don't know any monsters."

Suddenly she sat up straight, flapped the sheet down and nailed his eyes with an accusing glare. "He didn't care. Don't you see? He got me all hot and bothered, just showing off. I didn't matter to him. When I was panting, he just got up and walked away. I think he was punishing me. Can't you see that?"

Marsh released her wrists and shook his head, deep in thought.

Flouncing, turning onto her stomach, again putting her back to him, pulling the sheet up around her shoulders, Anna continued the account in a monotone. "He got another bucket of water and rinsed me off and he left, as if the whole thing had meant nothing to him."

Marsh's eyes roved over her form. The sheet dipped and swelled, following the line of her body. "Were you relieved when he left?" He was almost afraid of her answer.

She sputtered, strangling on her response. "You know what I really hate, Marsh?"

He didn't speak.

"What I really hate about you?"

He remained silent and unmoving.

"I hate you for knowing to ask me that."

She covered her head again with the sheet. "No, I was not relieved. You sitting there cool as a cucumber, you already knew the answer to that, too. I wanted him to keep touching me. And I loathed myself for that. I hated feeling like I needed him, for being so low—of having such awful weak character—that I looked forward to his coming every time, got excited about his coming back, no matter what he did to me."

Again her voice dropped. "Lord help me, I wanted him to stay. I yearned for him to keep making me feel like he made me feel, quivering with excitement, turned on like that."

Marsh waited.

"I am totally depraved." She rolled onto her back, flipped the sheet down, and peered at Marsh. Her eyes were wide, rimmed in red, frightened eyes.

"Marsh, I *wanted* him to come back. I *wanted* him to touch me like that. How could any decent woman have felt that way?" Her voice dropped. "The answer is, of course, no *decent* woman would have."

He could repeat the same answer he'd given her several times already, and thought that might be what she wanted, but she began talking again before he could remind her that none of this was her doing and that her responses were perfectly normal.

"When I heard him coming after that, I got butterflies in my stomach. I put the handcuffs on before he even told me to and got on my hands and knees. It was like I was inviting him.

"He lay down on his back and slid underneath me and I couldn't wait. When he touched me, I nearly swooned. When he finally sucked one of my breasts into his mouth, I practically fainted with pleasure."

She caught a quick glimpse of Joe, but didn't let her eyes linger. "Don't hate me for making me tell you this. Please don't hate me." She groaned. "I don't suppose it really matters if you do. You couldn't possibly hate me more than I hate myself."

A long silence settled between them before she spoke again. "My conscience or my innate sense of decency, kept throwing fits every time. Intellectually I didn't want him to do it, but when he did, it made me more excited than I've ever been before.

"Sometimes people in romance novels talk about exquisite torment, but I'd never experienced it. Not before."

Yes, Marsh had some knowledge of exquisite torment, but somehow experiencing the feeling was better than hearing about it. That kind of thing was only good if you were a participant. Foreplay was not a spectator sport.

"And how long did this go on?"

"I have no idea. He touched me and suckled and I loved it. Several times I tried to concentrate, tried not to like it, but I couldn't seem to stop."

"Okay, let's move on. What happened after he got through *suckling*?"

"He took off his clothes, but he stood where I couldn't see him. I kept my eyes closed anyway. I didn't want to see him. I had been able tell what he was doing. I heard clasps pop and his zipper. I asked him when he was going to let me go. He got still for a minute and I wondered if he had even thought that far."

Marsh didn't want to hear any more. But he was obligated. He only hoped hearing all of this didn't turn him into a raving maniac. Besides, if his new theory for her cure was right, he needed to know how far *he* needed to go to counter the damage the perp had done.

"Okay, so what happened, after he was undressed?"

"He draped himself over me from behind, like a dog mounting a bitch. It was degrading and I knew he was trying to beat me down, to make me an animal like him."

Marsh didn't notice the great crocodile tears until then, as they traced across her face.

"I was mortified to be manacled that way, like an animal forced to breed, or something.

"He rubbed himself up and down against me and I hated him more than I'd ever hated anyone or anything. I screamed and kicked, trying to get him off of me. I couldn't stand the thought of his worming his way inside me. I had a mental picture of how we looked at the moment and it was grotesque."

Her sobs made her breath convulse. Marsh moved closer and patted her arm in a helpless attempt to soothe her. He wanted her to keep talking, get all the way through it. She'd come this far. If they stopped now, he was afraid she might never get to this point again. She was spewing words like a broken water main and he doubted he could actually stop her if he tried.

"Even with all that, the awful, perverse side of me wanted him to...to do it...to force me.

"He backed away and began touching me there again, only this time with his hand instead of the sponge. I sat back so he couldn't reach me, but he wriggled his fingers underneath. He pinched me hard down there and I screamed. I told him—ordered him—not to hurt me. He lifted my bottom and I raised up a little so he wouldn't pinch me again. When I did what he wanted, he was gentle." She caught a quick breath. The tears had stopped.

"His being gentle with me...it made me cry. I was confused. I was thankful he wasn't hurting me, at the same time, I was disgusted, to think what we were doing, how we must look. Guilt and pleasure and fear and anger got all balled up together inside me and I began shaking.

"His fingers slid around in the wetness down there until I thought I might go crazy. He slapped my bottom to move me up and forward, and I thought he was going to rape me then.

"I wouldn't have fought him. I felt weird by then, like none of it was real, like I was absent and just watching. Truthfully, I had quit caring if he did it or not. It didn't matter. I was completely indifferent, holding the position he put me in like I was a robot or something.

"That's when he stopped. He hissed this weird little laugh, like the joke was on him, then he unlocked the cuffs and left."

She finally looked directly at Joe. "When he walked out that time...well, that was the worst moment of all." She exhaled, a hopeless sound. "I ached with wanting him, at the same time hating him, but someplace in that dark, perverse part of me, I decided I was probably starting to love him. We were alike, you see?" Her eyes appealed for understanding. "I wanted him to stay there with me. He could do anything to me he wanted, if he just wouldn't leave me alone there in that place anymore."

Her face twisted. "I know this all sounds completely screwy. That's why I couldn't tell anyone about it. How could I pass this nightmare on to my mother and dad? To my friends? To any other living person?" She looked startled, as if she just realized all over again that he, Marsh, was privy to the whole thing.

He managed a half smile, trying to reassure her that her secrets were safe with him and, at the same time, making similar promises to himself.

It wasn't his place to determine the rightness or wrongness of her behavior. Probably no one else who could put himself in her place would condemn her, but her perceptions of the reactions or thoughts of others were a different matter.

Joe had never been in a situation even remotely like hers. Few people had. Thank God.

Right now, he needed to get her all the way through her story. Later, they could decide what it would take to restore her to her former life, her former attitudes, her former innocence—if that were possible.

"I screamed and cried," she began again as Marsh nodded, encouraging her to continue. "I must have been venting all the hatred and frustration and anger. I was furious and I despised him for making me hate myself."

"And?"

Her chin quivered. "I decided to kill him." She tossed a quick glance at Marsh. "I had to, don't you see? Thinking that was the only way I could endure it. He knew about me, knew the whore that lived inside me; that she wanted him." She flinched at the thought of that. Then she gave out a low, keening wail. "I hated knowing that about myself, Marsh, and I promised myself that out of loyalty to me, I would never tell anyone. Maybe no one would guess. Maybe no one would be able to see inside or find out about...about me."

Her eyes rounded. Looking wild, they settled again on his face and she suddenly seemed to grow sad. Several moments passed before a half smile trembled at her mouth. "Now that you know, Marsh, in order to keep my secret, I guess I'll have to kill you and him, too."

He nodded agreement. "Okay. So, if I am one of only two people in the world who know your awful secret and you are going to murder me soon, I might as well hear the end of the story. What happened next?"

She lowered her eyes. "That was nearly the last time I saw him."

"Nearly?"

"When he came back, he told me not to put on the cuffs. I hadn't planned to, anyway. I was going to fight him. I was going to kill him or make him kill me, or at least drug me before I'd let him touch me again. I couldn't stand myself anymore anyway. One or both of us might as well be dead.

"Instead of the battle I thought was coming, he aimed the tranquilizing pistol at me through the bars, and fired.

"They found me asleep on the bench near the duck pond, fully clothed. And no one knew who he was or where he was. A couple of people—a police woman and her sidekick—tried to hint that the place and the perp had never really existed.

"I looked the same as I had fifty-three hours before— same hair, same clothes, same tissue in my pocket, same shoes—but I was changed, profoundly. Lord, how I was changed.

"The cop who found me asked for the man's description. I was woozy but I told him everything I could think of.

"They made me have a physical but the doctor who did the exam told my mother that I had not been sexually violated. I don't know the definition of the term 'sexually violated,' but I felt like I'd been pretty well defiled."

She threw her jean-encased legs over the side of the bed and rolled to a sitting position, swiping at the hair falling forward into her face.

"Then, suddenly, everyone started acting like the whole thing hadn't happened, except that I was missing fifty-three hours of my life. I had learned things in that time that I would never have suspected about myself—grotesque, evil, awful things; things I definitely did not want anyone else to know."

Joe watched her closely. "And that's why you refused to talk about it and turned down the counseling?"

"After I got fully awake, yes."

"How about talking to someone else who's qualified to help you, a woman counselor maybe, someone besides Dr. Ware?"

"No. If I were going to talk to any professional, it'd be him. He seems admirably indifferent. I like that about him— the detachment." She looked at Marsh as if she were startled. "Or you. I guess I could talk to you."

"Do I seem detached to you?"

Her answering smile wobbled. "Hardly."

"It's like you said, Anna, I don't have the training to give you the absolution you need."

She shrugged. "What absolution can there be for someone as depraved as I am?"

"You need to hear it from someone whose professional opinion you trust. From a doctor or your pastor. I keep telling you that your part in this is perfectly forgivable, but you aren't buying it from me. I imagine it's absolutely normal for anyone who endured what you did to feel guilty or afraid or even angry with yourself, but Anna, your reactions were all normal. We are sexual beings. Skillful titillation works on just about everyone."

She stared at him a long moment. "All I know is: I hoped they would never catch him. I don't want to have to testify against him in court. I don't want people asking questions, putting me on trial, judging me for my behavior. I don't want to have to look at him or smell him again ever."

"Smell him? Do you mean the yeast smell you mentioned before?"

"Yes. I haven't been able to go near a bakery. The smell is too...memorable."

Marsh saw the edge of sunlight peeping through the drapes in Anna's bedroom.

"Do you want to go back to sleep?"

Anna shook her head, tugging to straighten the jeans and T-shirt she'd worn since the day before which were badly rumpled and twisted.

Standing, Marsh moved back a step and offered her a hand up. Glowering from under furrowed brows, she put her hand in his and let him pull her to her feet.

He grinned. "I'll go get us some doughnuts. All that talk about yeast got me salivating." His appetite for food was not the only appetite stimulated by their conversation.

"I told you. I can't go near a bakery."

"Okay, but sooner or later, we're going to face all these ghosts. Why don't you rustle us up a pot of coffee while I'm gone."

She didn't say anything, but nodded as she headed toward the bathroom, still squirming and straightening her clothes.

He took a turn in the bathroom after Anna finished, shaved with a throwaway safety razor he found in the medicine cabinet, and made himself presentable.

After the difficult and time-consuming process of selecting doughnuts to please any palate, Joe located a pay phone. It was nearly 7 a.m. He called Police Lieutenant Ed

Archer at home, the man who had headed up the Fulenweider kidnap investigation.

"The man who abducted Anna Fulenweider smelled strongly of yeast," Marsh said, after the amenities.

"Yeah, we knew that. Got it from the patrolman who interviewed her before she clammed up. We checked grocery stores, bakeries, donut shops."

"How about the brewery?" Marsh hadn't remembered Anna's suggesting that possibility until that moment.

Archer was quiet on the other end of the line. "Yeah, okay. Good idea. I hadn't thought about brewer's yeast. Say, have you been able to pry any other information out of her?"

"Some."

"For instance?"

"The guy wore a disguise, like a clown costume or a harlequin."

At the other end of the line, Archer muttered. "Of course, he did."

"What?"

"They had a three-day school on campus, a school for rodeo clowns. Ran it out of the field house, which is directly across the parking lot from the performing arts center. Guys in clown make-up were everywhere. He could have gone almost anywhere on campus without drawing any special attention. She didn't mention to us that he wore a disguise."

"The field house?"

"Yeah. But, of course, we weren't looking around there. Since she was abducted from the parking lot, we assumed the perp had taken her as far away from there as he could get."

"By the way," Joe said, again curious, "who told you she was taken from the parking lot?"

Archer delayed a moment and Joe heard papers rustling. "It's here somewhere, in the initial report."

"Can you find out where that information came from?"

"Sure."

"I didn't realize you had an eye witness to the abduction."

"No, we don't. It came second- or third-hand."

"I think it might be important to know where that particular bit of information originated."

"I'll dig it up and let you know. Hey, Marsh, you're coming up with some very helpful stuff. Stay on her. We'll follow up on the brewery idea, the costume, the place where he grabbed her and anything else you get."

"Right. I'll have more today or tomorrow. She's just started opening up."

"Are you a psychologist? Is that how you're getting her to talk?"

"No. I'm a research engineer. Someone comes up with a gadget he needs and I design it for him."

Archer snorted a coughing laugh. "I guess we were barking up the wrong tree thinking a shrink could get through when what we needed was an engineer."

"Yeah, well, whatever works."

"Good point. How do we contact you?"

"You can call Fulenweider. She'll know where I am."

"Thanks, Marsh. We appreciate you keeping us in the loop. Not everyone does."

Driving back to Anna's condo, Marsh reviewed what he had learned earlier that morning.

Ware had said her guilt about her abduction was damaging her, but the good doctor didn't know what it was about. She had refused to help him figure it out. Now, Joe Marsh knew where that guilt was coming from but he didn't feel free to share what he'd learned...at least not yet. To keep her trusting him, he needed her permission to reveal those very private revelations to Ware. Now, how, exactly, was he going to go about getting that permission? He disliked being devious but, damn it, devious worked.

Chapter Sixteen

Joe dropped Anna at the Times. He would keep her car. Told her he had some errands to run, that he would pick her up for lunch.

Larry Grossbart supervised maintenance crews in the performing arts center and the field house which was adjacent. He and his people knew their way in and out of the power plant which operated from a basement connecting both facilities.

"I read every word they wrote about that deal," Grossbart said as he strode the hallway behind the temporary stage, an area littered with scenery and props used for campus events at the performing arts center. "There's no way a man could have hauled an unconscious woman out of here that afternoon without arousing a lot of curious people."

"How would you have done it, Larry, if you had wanted to make a full-grown woman disappear from this hallway?"

Grossbart coughed a light laugh. "You're not seriously thinking it was me or any of my crew."

"No, you've all checked out. The police know exactly where each of you was. I just need to pick your brain. Did you know about the peepholes in that closet."

"Shit, yes, I did. We dap those things about once a week, but the kids just punch new ones. It's worse in the ladies' locker room over at the field house. It's like trying to mend a break in a water hose. Once it gets started, they just keep popping open up and down the line."

"So, if some guy has his own peep show and gets all lathered up, how could he sneak an unwilling victim out of here?"

"You sure she wasn't willing?"

Joe tensed and made a determined effort not to overreact. "Yes."

"I saw her once, before it happened. Good-looking woman like that...well, I kind of got the idea that Fulenweider went along with him on her own, at least as far as the parking lot."

Marsh felt his temper rouse. How was it every guy he met mentioned she was good looking? Did every guy in town notice her? They had this whole campus full of babes to ogle. But he didn't want to go off after some red herring, so he reined in his annoyance in an effort to stay on task here. "Are you the one who told the police he took her from the parking lot?"

"No. How could I know that? I heard that's where she was and just figured she went along with him on her own steam. I hear she never did tell anyone much about it. What makes you think she didn't just go along?"

Marsh clenched his jaws. Grossbart looked like man with average intelligence but that was a dumbass question. Obviously he was just being candid, like he considered Joe something of an impartial observer.

Marsh answered Grossbart's question and suggestive leer with a gruff, "That isn't the way it happened. He chloroformed her in the closet with something and when she was out cold, he carted her off. What I'm trying to figure out is how he could have carried her without drawing a lot of attention and where to. It probably wasn't far. Now focus and look at it from that angle, will you?"

The maintenance supervisor sobered. "Sure. Okay." He looked around as if surveying the area for the first time. "Well, if I was going to do something like that, I suppose I'd toss something over her, like a blanket or a curtain or something, and I'd check to see that the coast was clear, then I'd carry her through that exit right there and down the stairs that are on the other side of that door." He pointed to a door at the end of the hallway. "That goes all the way down to the sub basement." He paused, regarding Marsh who was suddenly wide-eyed. Grossbart stammered. "Well, that's how I'd probably have done it."

Marsh stared at the well-marked exit Grossbart indicated, a door not thirty feet from the closet where Anna had been rendered unconscious. It would have been easy to do exactly as Grossbart described: wait for an opportunity, then hoist a bundle over his shoulder, slip down the hall, and through that door. With all the props around, no one would think anything of a workman with a bundle over his shoulder.

It would have been so damned easy. Marsh dealt in mechanical devices, not crime scenes, but even an amateur detective could figure this one out.

"It's not just a basement down there, either," Grossbart continued. "Well, the first level is basement, but under that, like I said, there's a sub basement below that one, which is really a utility tunnel."

"What do you mean, *tunnel*?"

"Runs the length and width of the campus."

"Really?"

"How do you think we keep the walkways clear and mostly dry between the buildings in icy weather?"

"I didn't know you did. How does that work?"

"Come on, I'll show you."

The sub basement/utility tunnel was exactly as Anna had described her prison. Machinery hummed in the distance, echoing off the walls. The sound definitely could be considered a drone. Steel poles, secured to cement floors, spanned the distance to the ceilings fifteen feet overhead. There were a series of chain-link fences, floor to ceiling, to cordon off hazardous areas.

"You know how college kids are," Grossbart offered when he noted Marsh's curious study of the facilities.

Yes, he knew. Could the perp have been some horny student, his condition made worse by peeping at scantily clad coeds darting around back stage and in the dressing rooms changing clothes?

Was Anna a random choice? Did the guy think he was ripping off some coed beauty queen?

Of course, Anna was better looking than some of the contestants Marsh had seen, but she was twenty-four years old, while most of them were eighteen-to-twenty.

He assumed the perp had snatched Anna specifically, that he was a man of discriminating tastes. It hadn't occurred to Joe that the kidnapper could be just some roustabout. Someone like Grossbart.

"How many people you got working for you, Grossbart?"

"Seven. Three women and four men. Wouldn't have women on the crews at all, but the university makes me hire 'em."

"You got something against women?"

The man gave him a weary smile. "I've got a wife and three daughters, mister. I'm here to tell you, that's all the women one man needs in his life."

Joe allowed a grudging smile. "Yeah, I suppose it would be."

They talked a few minutes longer before Joe let Grossbart return to his chores while Marsh walked briskly back to the exit door. He'd had an eerie feeling the first time he'd been through it with Grossbart. Could this be the door through which the perp had carried an unconscious Anna all those weeks ago?

After a tour below by himself, Marsh walked back to Anna's car. He wanted to talk to Dr. Ware and had new questions for Lieutenant Archer. He was concentrating as he walked, mulling over his findings, when Wesley wheeled into the parking lot. "Been looking for you."

Marsh gave him a wry smile. "Well, you found me. What's up?"

"Nothing. I just got to wondering what you were doing."

"Walking and thinking is most of it. I've been prowling around in the tunnels under the field house. Why didn't you tell me about those?"

"Didn't think about 'em. Why, do you think they've got something to do with Anna's kidnapping?"

Stemmons didn't seem to have any idea where Anna had been held captive. Of course, their mutual friend hadn't always been within earshot when she talked about it. Or maybe Lee hadn't paid attention. Maybe it was just that he didn't care where, as long as she was back. None of those possibilities seemed likely. But why would he withhold information that might help track down the guy who'd taken her? Obviously, he wouldn't.

Marsh chastised himself for being suspicious of every male she knew—practically of every man who ever laid eyes on her, from her boss at the paper, to the firemen who sneaked furtive glances at her, to the guy in charge of the university's physical plant. Then, too, there was Stemmons. And even good old Dr. Ware, a man old enough to be her grandfather but not too old to appreciate her.

Taking the initiative, Lee followed Marsh downtown to the police station where Joe suggested Archer get a map of the utility tunnels and look for some outlet near a bakery, someplace the perp might work or live that would give him access to the tunnels.

Wesley insisted on following again when Marsh went to see the psychiatrist, then rankled when Dr. Ware excused him.

"I'm the guy who brought Marsh into this in the first place," Stemmons objected. Obviously he wanted to hear their conversation.

Dr. Ware was kindly, but insistent. "You are a close friend of hers, Wesley. This information would not be easy for you to hear."

"What about Marsh?"

"Apparently, she has opened up some to him."

"I should be able to know anything he knows. Why shouldn't I?"

Ware was patient but firm as he escorted Wesley into the reception room. "Well, for instance, you might be tempted to take action on your own, if and when we find this man. Also, Anna might not want you to know. If she did, she probably would have confided in you during the last few weeks, don't you think?"

It was a rhetorical question and the doctor didn't wait for a response. "Now, if you'd like something to drink, my secretary will be glad to get it for you. We shouldn't be long. I may not hear all of Joe's information, myself."

Blustering, saying he saw no reason to cool his heels in Ware's reception room, Wesley swelled to his full height and left the office in a huff.

They hadn't been together long when Ware quietly interrupted Joe's account to call Lieutenant Archer. When he had the investigator on the line, Ware suggested the police keep an eye on Anna now that she was talking. Her revelations might threaten the perp, who quite naturally was interested in preserving his anonymity.

Ware then continued listening intently as Marsh relayed all that Anna had told him.

"She's afraid of seeing him again," Ware speculated, late in the interview.

Joe said, "I agree, but what's she afraid of?"

"I'm not sure about her specific fear, but I can tell you, it would be the best therapy in the world for her to see him in custody. To get free of this, to get closure, she needs to confront the situation, her own behavior, and the perpetrator, face-to-face, on equal footing, when she's not at a disadvantage."

Ware paced around his desk to settle in the chair next to Joe. "You've done yeoman's work here, Marsh. I know it's hard to maintain your objectivity, but you have done an exemplary job so far. The thing is, you've got to keep on doing it." He gave Joe a stern, fatherly look, which warmed him and made the younger man smile.

Ware seemed to assume Joe's agreement as he continued. "You've walked her through the hardest part, made her recall what happened and speak openly about her disappointment at her own responses. You were right to assure her that her sensuality was a normal reaction as, of course, it was.

"Now, you have to hold your point of progress and continue from there until the police turn up the villain."

"What if they don't?"

"Keep the dialogue with her open. Encourage her to recall every insignificant little detail. She's purging the experience and it's cleansing her. Maintain your momentum. Don't let up. You've established a beachhead, plant the flag and set up a field camp. Make the site your home. You need to make this psychological arena easy for her to stroll in and out of. Do you see what I mean?"

"Yes, sir, I think so. But shouldn't you be doing this instead of me?"

"If she'll let me, but the main thing is to keep the communication channel open and flowing. Keep encouraging her to come talk to me. I've told my people that I am available to Anna anytime she calls or wants to come in. But don't let it sound like you're trying to palm her off on me because you're losing interest."

Marsh shivered at the suggestion. "Fat chance. She's established a beachhead of her own, right in here." Joe patted his ribs in the area of his heart. "Talk about setting up a base camp. She's gotten to me, Doc. I'm starting to like her way too much. I don't want my needs to burden her, but it's a real strain keeping my *interest* under control."

"Then don't. It will be good for her to see your natural regard growing." He offered a mischievous grin. "My advice is: let it all hang out."

Joe chuffed, a half laugh/half cough. "I don't think you get it. What's festering in me has got nothing to do with *regard*. It's lust, Doc, pure and simple."

"Then I should imagine those inclinations will give you additional insights into the perp's thinking."

Joe's shoulders slumped. "He made her feel dirty. I don't want to do that."

"When you assured her that her sensual responses were normal, were you telling her the truth? Were her responses normal?"

"Well sure." Joe paused. "That's right, isn't it?"

"Yes, it is. She likes you, doesn't she, Joe? Do you think she is as physically attracted to you as you are to her?"

Marsh pursed his mouth and nodded. "I don't mean to sound immodest, but yeah, I think she is attracted, just maybe not as much as I am to her." He added as an aside, "I don't hardly see how she could be."

"Then maybe you should let her experience some of those same sensual responses with you. Show her they're not *dirty*, but perfectly normal. Wholesome. Encourage her to think of those kinds of sensations as something to be savored and enjoyed; as feelings that can be very, very pleasant."

Marsh glared at Ware, not able to believe what the good doctor had just suggested. "Don't give me permission to hustle her, Doc, because that's what my gut's been telling me to do. I've been scared to death of setting her back, of sending her skittering into that hell hole she's been struggling so hard to get out of."

"Go with your instincts, Joe. I assume you're familiar with her body language now. Wouldn't you agree?"

Marsh narrowed his eyes. "Yeah, I'd say so."

"She hated to have you touch her at first, but she likes for you to touch her now, doesn't she?"

Joe yielded a confident smile. "That is true."

"Then hold the ground you've got and proceed. Conquer each emotional plateau in slow, steady steps. Progress one level at a time."

"Are you talking about physical intimacy? Am I hearing you right?"

Ware studied Joe thoughtfully for a long moment. "What do you think?"

Marsh began laughing. "I think I might make a pretty fair shrink myself, Doc, if lusting after Anna Fulenweider is one of the requirements. I might be more inclined to pay my patients than charge for the work, though."

Ware chuckled at Joe's taunting grin. "My oath prevents my doing that part of her therapy although I, too, find her very attractive, and that encompasses more than just her physical appearance." He gave Marsh an understanding pat. "You're making progress with her partly because you genuinely like her and she interprets that as approval. Approval counts for a lot with her right now. I care but I wasn't able to convince her to let me help her. You were. Still, I'm ready to jump in and try, if and when she'll let me. Are you afraid to push on with this?"

"Hell, no, I'm not afraid."

"Are you afraid it will lead to an unwanted personal attachment or a commitment of some kind on your part?"

"Not exactly."

The doctor eyed him warily, and Marsh exhaled. "I'll try to get her to come see you, Doc. It might be I'll have to tell her I've clued you on some of it. She thinks her behavior was too bad to tell you about, that you wouldn't understand or be able to forgive her." He waved his hand, preventing Ware's interruption. "I already asked her what you'd have to forgive her for, and she said for being who it turned out she was when she was with this guy."

"And we already know what that's about, don't we?"

"She hasn't forgiven herself?"

"Exactly. She's damaged her image of herself. We have to help her regain that flagging self respect. But at least she didn't flatly refuse to come this time."

"Right."

"That's good progress, Marsh. That's a whole lot further than we've gotten in the past."

Marsh was up and moving toward the door before he stopped abruptly. "There haven't been any other kidnappings, have there, Doc? Is this our perp's one-time crime?"

Strolling to open the office door, Ware hesitated with his hand on the knob. "It's likely he will do it again, eventually."

"It's been a couple of months since he took her."

"The main problem being that he was successful the first time." Ware stared at the sculpted design in the carpet. "He might be watching her. If he is, he could still be riding the high of having battered her this way. Fulenweider is an attractive, intelligent woman. Until she is well, she's still under his influence almost as much as she was when she was under his actual physical control. If he's watching her, he may know that. It's obvious she still suffers from his influence."

Marsh clenched his jaws and his fists in unison. "And I feel it, too. Damn him, anyway."

"Don't let it gnaw at you. You've got to stay immune to his influence."

"I don't know why I should care about me falling under his influence."

"Oh, I think you do. I think we both do."

Sullen, Marsh walked out of Ware's office but turned back and noticed that the older man was smiling and looking a little self-satisfied.

Chapter Seventeen

Joe tried to shake off his new agitation before he picked Anna up for lunch.

"I have the afternoon off again," she said, as he drove. He glanced at her. There was something different. She added, "So, what do you want to do?"

He slanted another look at her from the corner of his eye. "I don't know. What would you like to do?"

Instead of answering directly, she posed another question. "Marsh, do you consider us friends?"

Something about her demeanor made the hair bristle along the back of his neck. "Yes," he said cautiously.

"I can trust you. Am I being naive about that, or is that correct? Can I trust you?"

"Well, yes. Of course. I thought you knew..."

"But can I trust you as I have never trusted another living soul?"

"I think so. Yes."

"Would you be willing to spend this afternoon doing anything I wanted to do and then forget it completely?"

"I guess so." He was feeling better but the bristling neck hair remained on alert.

She took a deep breath and bit both lips, but she seemed reluctant to tell him what was on her mind.

"Come on," he prodded. "Don't agonize about it. Just say it. What is it you want to do?"

She clasped her hands in her lap and glared at them. "I think I might have some internal, mental deformity." She looked at him suddenly. "Marsh, I dream about him. Erotic dreams. In a very perverse way, I liked the sensations he...well...introduced."

Marsh moved the car into the slow lane so he could pay better attention. "Anna, have you dated much?"

"Probably as much as most women my age."

"I mean, have you ever been serious about anyone?"

"If you mean, have I wanted to marry anyone, no."

He didn't like beating around this bush. "What I mean is: have you been intimate with a man?"

Her fair skin turned rosy from the collar of her blouse up. "Define *intimate.*"

"Petting. Have you done any serious petting?"

"The kind that requires taking your clothes off?"

"Yes."

"Not exactly." Her mouth twisted as if she were ashamed. "What I mean is, not really. Not until...him."

Marsh tried to appear confident, like he knew what he was doing. Doctor's orders, he reminded himself, and he risked a quick peek at her. Pretty tough assignment, but someone had to do it.

"Let's go to your place for lunch," he suggested, testing, curious to see where that idea took them.

"A bologna sandwich?"

"Or P.B. and J. I'm not finicky."

She laughed lightly. "And I can slip into something more comfortable."

"If you want to." He was picking up some pretty unbelievable vibes from her broad hints. Broad hints from a broad. Good one.

"I mean, I could put on something more...ah...casual."

He had the idea. She didn't have to beat him over the head with it. Oh, yeah, he was pretty sure he knew what she was getting at. He just wasn't sure that *she* knew.

She eyed him suspiciously. "What do you think we could do with a free afternoon?"

He grinned. Oh, yeah, she was getting it. "I'm sure we could put our heads together; think of something that'll satisfy both of us."

She gave him a timid smile and his neck hair quivered with heightened anticipation.

At her apartment, Joe closed the front door and flipped the deadbolt. They might be needing a little privacy.

Striding toward her bedroom, Anna said, "Do you want to start making the sandwiches? I'll help as soon as I get my clothes changed." She was going for a diversion, chickening out maybe.

"No."

"What?" She looked more curious than alarmed, as she pivoted and set her somber gaze on him.

"I want to help you." He stepped close to her.

She didn't shrink from him, but set her eyes on his moving hand, a rabbit mesmerized by a rattler. "What do you mean?"

He watched her face carefully as he touched the top button on her blouse, the one just below her throat.

Her breathing quickened and the flush deepened.

He moved deliberately. There was more riding on this than the usual turn-on.

Staring into his face, she didn't flinch as he freed the first button. A sigh produced a tiny moan behind her closed lips as he ran his index finger down the placket to undo the second button. Cautiously, he opened her blouse just enough to see the swell of her breasts before they rolled into the seclusion of her bra.

Keeping a tight leash on his own skyrocketing feelings, Joe unfastened two more buttons, then used both his hands to tug her shirttail out, giving him access to the last one.

When her blouse hung open, he pushed the sides away and took a step back to get a full look at her. She didn't speak or try to retreat as she studied his face, obviously watching for his reaction to what he saw.

He tried to smile with just a hint of intrigue. "Your turn," he said quietly, and stepped close again.

When she stared at him, obviously uncertain about his meaning, he caught one of her hands and lifted it to the top button on his shirt.

Looking surprised and maybe relieved, she unbuttoned his shirt slowly, tugged the shirttail out of his slacks and finished, then brushed both sides away and looked at his bare torso, which she had seen before, the day they met, the morning when he was wearing only a towel.

He grinned. "Naughty girl, what are you thinking?"

Her eyes flashed with excitement or apprehension or both and she laughed, a throaty rumbling that sounded slightly sinister before she said, "Now what do we do?"

"Let's get naked."

Her large, dark eyes rounded and she stumbled back several steps, shaking her head.

Joe froze, afraid if he reached to steady her, he would frighten her.

She glanced at the open door to her bedroom, then back at him, as if she were calculating her chances of putting herself safely behind that door's lock.

Instead of moving toward her, he retreated, sat down on the sofa, crossed an ankle over a knee, and rested one arm on the back cushion. "Come sit for a minute. Take a load off."

She watched him as his cocker spaniel had when Joe was a kid, cocking her head slightly to one side in an obvious attempt to comprehend what was happening.

Clocks ticked, but she stood unmoving, her blouse gaping open, staring at the floor. Joe finally stirred first, got up and walked toward her, extending a hand. She slid her hand into his and he tugged her back to the sofa. He waited until she sat, then settled beside her.

Keeping his elbows firmly against his sides as a safety precaution, Joe dusted an easy, non-threatening kiss across her lips. She didn't flinch or respond, didn't even move, at first.

Then, staring at him, looking both pained and accusing, she leaned closer, opened her mouth slightly, and set her lips over his.

She smelled good, and tasted better, and... She wilted against him and he almost forgot his mission entirely, only retained control by concentrating on keeping his elbows to his sides. Good idea, he praised himself. His underarms and his upper lip were perspiring. Those were not good signs. Steeling himself, he was holding his own until Anna began to wriggle. He risked a quick peek.

She was removing her blouse, but the wriggling didn't stop with that. Her ample breasts fell free from their lacy harness and she tossed her bra on the floor beside her blouse.

He had to control himself and this situation. He had to, he chided. But that thought was before she smashed her bare upper body against his naked chest.

His elbows broke free of his mental anchor. With one hand at either side of her waist, he lifted to scrub her softness against the mat of hair that covered his chest and stomach. He deepened the kiss, claiming her, marking her as his own as her naked upper body melted against his.

She put her arms over his shoulders and ran her fingers into the hair on the back of his head, setting off fireworks inside, fireworks that threatened to burn the slim thread of control to which he clung.

Suddenly, she whined, set her hands at his shoulders and shoved herself away from him. He allowed the separation without thinking.

"What is it?" he mumbled, struggling to break out of the erotic dream.

"Will you lie down on the floor?" she asked.

His mind didn't seem to be functioning worth a damn, but if she wanted him on the floor, that's where he'd be. He thought idly how compliant he'd become. When Anna Fulenweider told Joe Marsh to jump, she didn't have to say it twice.

Shrugging free of his shirt, he dropped to the floor on his stomach, ready to give her push-ups, if that's what she wanted.

"Roll over," she whispered. "Lie on your back."

He was beginning to get an idea about where this was going. He did as she said, then stared in disbelief as she dropped to her hands and knees beside him.

She couldn't seem to look at him. He closed his own eyes as she moved, positioning herself directly over him. He felt the heat of her, smelled her fragrance, heard how rapid her breathing became. But he had to be still. He had to wait for orders. Nothing. He must do nothing on his own.

Her voice rasped. "Touch me...please."

Her oversized breasts filled his hand as he caressed them one at a time, so round, so firm, so fully packed...he recalled the lines of an old advertising jingle.

He fondled her until his groin throbbed. Then, she relaxed her rigid back, dropping her breasts closer to his face and wheezed a new command. "Could you please...? Marsh, will you...?"

He knew what she wanted and caught one teasing nipple carefully between his lips.

The woman poised above him gasped and froze a long moment as he suspended all movement. Slowly, she began to writhe. She pulled that nipple from his mouth—producing a smucking sound—only to present the other one.

As he suckled, his hands caressed her, gliding over bare skin until she was panting and needy and lowering herself, wordlessly asking for more.

"Oh, God, help me...be...good," she whined.

At her plea, Joe rolled, lifting her as he moved until he was positioned above her. She rocked her head from side and side moaning, then wheezing, "I'm sorry. Marsh, I'm so sorry. I am so bad." She moaned, a low, mournful sound. She lay tormented, refusing to look at him, until her breathing slowed to its earlier steady rhythm. Joe was delighted not to see any sign of the palsy that had come over her so unexpectedly before.

He concentrated on his facial expression, wanting to make it right, knowing she would be trying to read his thoughts.

It seemed ironic. Instead of realizing all this innate passion was a gift from God, she seemed to think it originated in Hell. He knew women who never experienced an orgasm, not with any man. Here was a beautiful, charming nymph who had no idea she held a marvelous, God-given gift of sensuality. But he wasn't going to let it remain a secret long. It was not only his duty, but his privilege.

The doorknob on the front door rattled. "Hey, who in the hell locked this door?"

It was Wesley.

Anna pushed at Joe's stomach and chest, scrambling wildly, in a panic.

Moving quickly, Marsh stood and pulled her to her feet in one smooth, easy motion. Bending, he swept her bra and blouse up in one hand, squeezed her arm to make her more alert and pushed her gently toward her bedroom.

It sounded like Wesley was beating on the door with both fists. He shouted as if the world was on fire.

"Quiet down," Marsh said, cramming his arms into his shirtsleeves as he hurried to the door. He glanced back. Things looked fine. Their activity on the floor hadn't mussed anything. He buttoned his shirt then slipped the deadbolt.

Wesley burst into the room. "Where is she? What have you done to her? Marsh, if she's hurt, I'll kill you, man, with my bare hands. I swear it." He darted into the kitchen and looked around frantically. "Where is she?"

"In her room, Lee. She's in her bedroom. She might have been asleep. Of course, I doubt she is now, after your grand entrance."

Wesley shot a look at Marsh, then did a double take and his eyes narrowed. "And where were you, Marsh? Were you in the bedroom with her?"

"No. I haven't been invited into her bedroom yet. Have you?"

Wesley sputtered then, unable to speak, he gestured up and down Joe's shirt. "Then what's this about?"

Joe looked down. His shirt was buttoned wrong.

"I was just checking myself out, in the mirror, in the bathroom." He grimaced. "And, no, she wasn't in the bathroom with me."

Wesley took a deep breath but continued scowling at his friend for a long moment before he sighed. "She's mine, man. I look out for what's mine. That's what you're doing here, looking out for what's mine. You understand?"

It was Joe's turn to sigh. "That's exactly what I'm doing, Lee, trying to look out for Anna. But, my friend, she doesn't have a clue that she belongs to you."

"But you know it," Stemmons said. "You understand that, don't you?"

Marsh shrugged and blinked. "Do you want her to get well?"

"What the hell is that supposed to mean?"

"If you want her to get well, you'll have to let me do whatever it takes to make her well. If you want her cowed, trembly, dependent on you, then I'd better leave right now."

Wesley looked alarmed. "What are you talking about, man? You're making real progress. I talked to Dr. Ware on the phone, just before I came over here. He thinks maybe you can pull this off."

Joe nodded. "I do too, but you may lose her in the process. Can you live with that?"

A slow smile flickered on Stemmons' face. "Nah, man. I swear she won't be able to keep from loving me when she's

her old self again. I'd do anything for her." His voice
dropped. "I already have. Who could resist someone who
loves 'em as much as I love her? It's not even possible."

Moving toward the kitchen, Joe shook his head,
frowning at nothing in particular.

"So, what'd you guys have for lunch," Wesley said, chatty
and friendly as Anna emerged from the bedroom looking
flushed as if she just gotten up.

She avoided looking at Marsh until Wesley asked about
lunch, then she shot Joe a guilty warning glance. Reading
the look, he chuckled.

"We got busy establishing our ground rules and forgot to
eat."

Wesley groaned. "You all got to quit arguing all the time.
It keeps you too stirred up. Look at 'er, Joe, she can't hardly
bring herself to set her eyes on you. Why you gotta keep 'er
in a frenzy all the time?"

Joe and Anna looked at each other. Their eyes locked
and they began laughing into each other's faces.

"That's more like it," Stemmons said with a grin. "Now
you two kiss and make up."

Joe started toward Anna who turned on her heel beating
a hasty retreat toward the kitchen. Wesley's eyes rounded
and he flattened a big hand in the middle of Joe's chest.
"That was just a figure of speech and you know it."

Joe smirked at Anna who was peering through the pass-
through between the living room and the kitchen.

"That's one of my biggest faults, Lee, taking things too
literally. Isn't that right, Anna?"

She flashed him a secret smile and opened the
refrigerator door, either to find something to eat, or to hide
behind. He wasn't sure which.

Chapter Eighteen

"I don't like leaving you two alone," Wesley said, after they had eaten the chicken enchiladas, the spinach salad, and most of the butterscotch brownies. "The way you're at each other's throats and that.

"Of course, at the same time, you see, Grandridge and I know the kind of pictures we need, which means I'm the only man that can deliver on this assignment. But, Joe, I want your solemn word of honor that you're gonna behave yourself."

"All right."

"Do I have it?"

"Yes."

"And you will do anything she says and do it with a smile on your face, right?"

Marsh didn't know if he should, but he shot a quick glance at Anna who dropped her eyes rather than meet his gaze.

Marsh wasn't going to let her off that easily. "What about her? Doesn't she have to do everything I say with a smile on her face?"

"No way, man. And quit thinking what we all know you're thinking. You are one high-risk bodyguard, I'll say that."

Joe waggled his eyebrows up and down. "Depends on the body, Lee. I definitely would sacrifice mine to save hers, and that's a take-it-to-the-bank guarantee."

He looked at Anna, who was staring at him wide-eyed, and winked. She grimaced, hiding the smile, but he heard the muffled giggle and couldn't help grinning too.

Joe and Anna remained seated in their places at the small dining table, speculating about the weather, as Stemmons disappeared into the bathroom, then returned. On his way out, he admonished them again. "Remember, I want you to play nice while I'm gone."

"Yes, sir, Boss," Joe said, giving him a cross-eyed look and a silly salute with his left hand.

After Wesley's departure, neither Joe nor Anna seemed eager to be the first to splinter the amnesty of silence between them.

Finally, she said, "He likes me."

Joe surrendered a kindly smile. "Yeah, he does."

She shook her head and winced. "Obviously he doesn't really know me."

"It's knee-jerk. He responds to you like a lot of men do, Anna. To your beautiful bod, your face, your big, undiscriminating smile."

Her eyes rounded as she lifted her unbelieving glance to his face. "What about you?"

He chuckled quietly, folded his napkin beside his empty plate, slid his chair back from the table, and stood. "Sure. I do too. I'm a normal, red-blooded American male. Haven't you noticed?"

Skeptically, she watched him. "Are you going to tell Dr. Ware everything you wheedled out of me?"

He eased onto the sofa and patted the cushion next to him, wordlessly inviting her to join him. Instead, she walked to the middle of the floor and sat down facing him, sitting Indian style. He shrugged, content to be in the same room.

"First," he began, "I didn't *wheedle* anything out of you or coerce you, and you damn well know that."

She glowered at him and he arched his eyebrows.

"I did not. You needed to talk. I think you knew talking to me would help. And it has. You just didn't have anyone around you felt you could trust with your story until I showed up." He put up a hand to stop her argument. "I mean anyone you trusted to keep liking you after they heard your *sordid tale*."

She stared at the floor, so he continued.

"I think when we met face-to-face at Lee's the other morning, you figured I was the kind of guy who plays fast and loose and that helped."

Her face twisted into a hard frown. "My story is sordid, Marsh, for innocent ears," she said, latching onto and taking issue with his opening statement. If that's what she wanted to discuss, he would cooperate.

"So far what you've told me only indicates you are normal, Anna," he began. "Okay, so you can be sexually aroused. That only proves you've got healthy, normal responses to stimuli, sweetheart, not that you're perverse. You are a beautiful woman. Beautiful women excite men. You inspire us, make us dream dreams and reach beyond our limitations to conquer worlds and build empires."

She looked concerned. "But not you."

"Yes, me. Of course me. What do you think, that I'm some inferior being? If you were...well...in condition, I'd spend every minute we had alone trying to charm my way into your undies. You make me crazy." He looked apologetic. "But it's no good two of us being nuts, right? And it's still your turn...for the time being."

"I'm not crazy."

He settled an unbelieving look on her. "Well, finally. I'm glad to hear you say that. That statement alone makes me feel like we are making progress."

"What do you mean?"

"I think you've been protecting yourself by hiding behind the possibility you might be mentally challenged about your experience, using that wounded dove routine to fend off family, friends, other guys, and questions."

"But not you?"

"Right. Not me. I like you too much to let you get away with that dodge."

"Does that mean you are going to tell Dr. Ware?"

"Yes. And you want me to, don't you? You do know you need and want his professional advice."

She gave him a hard look, then just as he thought she was about to smile, she nodded.

"Actually, Anna, it'd really be more efficient for you to spill your guts to him direct. Why won't you?"

"Because I didn't want him to know...how I was...am."

"What? that you're a hot-blooded babe who didn't know she was until some stranger came along to show her a dimension of herself that she didn't know existed? That's what you don't want Ware to know?"

"You make it sound like my behavior was a good thing."

He grinned broadly. She was beginning to understand. All she needed was validation, someone to assure her that her responses were normal.

He lowered his voice. "You are a beautiful woman, Anna. Being naive makes you sexy. I don't have to tell Dr. Ware that. He already knows. You exude appeal, like a old-timey radiator warms a room. It's subtle, but it gets the job done with little fanfare.

"Yes, I plan to tell Dr. Ware everything you've told me, because I want me to. And he's going to tell you exactly what I have. Furthermore, I'm going to share some of the things you've told me with Lieutenant Archer, things that will help him track this jerk."

"And Wesley?"

He stared at her a long moment, trying to read her preference.

"No. Lee's vulnerable where you're concerned. He doesn't need any additional pressure."

"He'll know you're not telling him everything. He'll try to drag it out of you."

Joe suddenly felt relieved. He'd guessed right. She didn't want him to share what he knew with Lee. "Listen, woman, I'm every bit as tough as you are. If he hasn't dragged it out of you, there's no chance he'll get it from me. If you want him in the loop, you'll have to put him there." He eyed her thoughtfully. "Why haven't you told him any of the details?"

"I...I didn't want him to know about me either."

"What, that you were hot to trot. He'd have been tickled pink to help you ease that raging libido, kid."

"But, Marsh..." Her voice broke. "I don't want him to do it." She ducked her head, obviously embarrassed or ashamed. "I don't feel that way about him."

Reading her body language, his instincts honed to the ready, Joe lowered his voice. "I know you don't." He gave an embarrassed laugh. "The truth, of course, being: you want me. And we'll work that out. I promise. Just as soon as we get you steady on your feet emotionally."

Her eyes narrowed as she studied him and he gave her his best, most seductive grin. "I am what you want, aren't I, Anna?"

A half smile twitched the corners of her mouth, but she didn't say yes or no.

Marsh's grin broadened.

Lee was gone less than an hour, during which time Joe and Anna talked and cleaned up the supper dishes together, laughing into each others' faces and touching casually as they brushed by one another in a doorway or worked side-by-side in the small kitchen.

"What did she say about me?" Wesley's idle question had a note of urgency as he and Marsh drove back to Stemmons' apartment that night.

"She trusts you, Lee. She values your friendship. She isn't interested in getting romantically involved with you."

Stemmons glowered. "You mean with me specifically, or with any guy?"

"With anyone, right now."

"But you think she'll be normal again, don't you?"

"Yes. But I don't think she's ever going to be interested in you, buddy, even then."

Wesley stiffened and drew a deep breath. "Well, don't bet the farm on it, *buddy*."

Lieutenant Archer had left a message on Wesley's machine. He wanted Joe to call him at home.

"Is Stemmons with you?" Archer asked after Joe had identified himself.

"Yes."

"Don't react or repeat what I tell you."

"Okay."

"I tracked down the source of the information about her being abducted from the parking lot."

"Where'd it come from?"

"Stemmons."

Joe had to concentrate to keep from looking at Wesley. "Where'd he get it?"

"He said it came from a guy who'd been hanging around the parking lot while the cops were interviewing people."

"Did he give you a name?"

"He said he didn't get one."

"How about a description."

"Nope."

"Okay."

"Marsh, that piece of information misled us. If we'd known she'd been abducted from inside the building, we would have started our investigation there instead of running all over campus."

"Yeah. I can see how that might have been a problem."

"It was a red herring, plain and simple. Stemmons said he'd seen too many faces that day. And he seemed genuinely upset. Said he couldn't give us any kind of a description. The guy he saw might have been the perp. Indirectly feeding us bad info might have kept us from finding him...and her."

"Yeah."

"I need to talk to Stemmons, but the new information you got from her raised another thought. An ugly one."

"Yeah, I follow."

"I know he's your friend and all."

"Say no more. I'll follow up and check in with you later."

Marsh hung up the phone and turned to his friend. "Lee, what'd the guy look like, the one who said he'd seen Anna kidnapped out of the parking lot?"

Stemmons looked startled before he regained control of his expression, but Marsh had seen enough.

Wesley hedged. "What are you talking about, man?"

"Archer checked back to see where that lead came from. He said it came from you."

"That's wrong. He got it from one of his own cops."

"Both the campus and the city cops say you told them some guy had told you that."

"I guess they just forgot." He sneered. "That's so typical of cops, trying to cover their tails for not getting an i.d. on the guy. It wasn't me."

"Did you see people in clown make-up and costumes around campus while Anna was missing?"

"Yeah. Men and women both. There was a school for rodeo clowns going on. They were dressed up in that gear everywhere. All over town."

"Hmmm." He wanted to give Stemmons a little rope. "I thought maybe one of them might have been who told you they saw her"

"No, man, I told you, it didn't come from me."

"If you say so."

Wesley set his jaw. "I say so."

"Okay, don't be so defensive. I guess it was just a misunderstanding."

Later, however, when Marsh tried Wesley's denial on Archer, the lieutenant wasn't buying.

"These campus police guys may not be seasoned cops, but both of the ones involved in this are very sharp, very observant college students thinking to get into law enforcement or law school. They would not both be that far wide of the target."

"Okay." Marsh set his mind busily scanning for possibilities. An honest mistake? Could be. He didn't want to consider the one possibility that wandered through his mind when he let his thoughts run unguarded.

Wesley was infatuated. There's no way he would hurt her, at least not intentionally. But who would have suspected that the arrogant, self-assured reporter might be hung-up about her own sexuality? Or that she would be so virginal?

"You're not telling me everything, are you, Marsh?" Wesley asked that night.

"No, I'm not."

"I brought you into this, man. You owe me."

"Some of it is crap and you don't need to hear it. It might make you crazy, like I can promise you it's making me."

"So, if you can handle it, I can."

"No, man. I wish I didn't know some of it. I'm trying to forget it as soon as I pass it along. Actually, I'm just serving as a kind of conduit from her to Ware, getting the information for him to use to help her."

"What's he saying?"

"He says she's injured right now. He wants to minimize the extent of the long-term damage, that's what. You're too close to her. Too good a friend. She might need to confide in you. If you already knew stuff, you might tip your hand." Marsh glanced down. "Hey, what is that on your hands?"

Wesley clenched both fists and lowered them to his sides. "It's the chemicals. Messing with developer caused me to get psoriasis."

Joe figured his imagination was probably working overtime, but he recalled Anna saying her kidnapper's hands felt calloused, in spite of the latex gloves. What if they weren't calloused at all, but roughened by a scaly outcropping of psoriasis?

Come on, man, Joe chided himself mentally. *You want her, but not this way. She'll be the last one, the hardest to convince it could be him.*

Marsh glanced at Wesley. The man would have had a lot of advantages, if he wanted to grab Anna and have her all to himself for a time, completely at his mercy.

But Lee was too much of a ladies' man to do something like that. If the urge got that strong, he would have found some other, willing female.

Lee came from a long line of male chauvinists. His dad had put his mom out working the street as a prostitute to make extra money when the family needed income. She complained loud and long. Joe remembered a bad scene or two.

But Lee had more regard for women than his dad and his uncles did. Besides, he was crazy about Anna. No. The idea of his using her sexually was preposterous.

Wesley glanced at Joe, then did a double take. "Why're you looking at me like that, man?"

"That's my thinking look." Joe tried to give him a sheepish grin. "You just wound up on the receiving end of it, that's all."

"Well get that thing under control and point it a different direction."

Nodding, Joe attempted another smile, and tried to shake off his eerie suspicions.

Chapter Nineteen

Anna walked to the door leading into the photo lab and called Wesley's name as she scanned a damp photo flopping in her hand.

"Wesley," she called again, "this one's fuzzy. Can you...?"

There was no answer and none of the machines hummed, as they usually did when Stemmons or one of the other photographers was working.

She wandered in, lured by the light. Usually the red lights cast shadows in the short hallway and spooked her, but today the overheads were on.

The place smelled distinctly of the chemicals staff photographers used to develop their pictures.

Wesley always kept his area neat, the drawers and cabinets meticulously locked. As Anna looked around, she noticed one little padlock hanging open on the proof drawer. Maybe he had another print of this particular car accident. Wesley protected his work zealously, but it wasn't like she was one of his competitors. He and she were on the same team. A sharper picture would bode better for them both.

She slid the drawer open and used her index finger to push the top few prints out of her way. Beauty queens, for crying out loud. Didn't he get bored snapping all those... WHOA! One of the lovelies was nude.

Anna's eyes popped wide.

These were pictures of the girls in the most recent contest. Posing nude was a no-no, a sure way to get a contestant disqualified. Moral turpitude was one of the points the contest people stressed. That and the girls' public images and behavior.

In the past, some had posed privately, which only worked if they didn't get caught. But surely none of these girls would have modeled for a news hound like Wesley with his connections to mass communication.

Anna picked up a handful of the pictures and began shuffling through, studying them more closely.

The girls were not lounging in provocative poses. These ladies were standing up and in various stages of undress, disrobing or putting on clothes.

One or two daredevil contestants might take such a risk, but not what, five, six of them? No way.

Negatives of the roll were paper-clipped to the last picture. One by one, Anna held the negatives toward the overhead light.

She stopped when she came to one who was not standing, but lying down, on her stomach, her arms high over her head, her mouth gaping as if she were asleep. The reversal made it hard to identify which one it was.

She appeared to be on the ground. The shape looked vaguely familiar, even in the reverse lighting of the negative.

Anna suddenly gasped and clamped the handful of negatives against her.

It couldn't be. Where had these come from? Had Wesley found the pervert and confiscated these filthy pictures to protect her?

No, even giving it her most generous interpretation, Anna knew that wasn't the explanation.

Shaking her head from side to side, denying her own conclusion before it could become a conscious thought, Anna shot out of the dark room, stumbling over the threshold as she rocketed through the short hallway and back into the newsroom.

Her eyes rolled, sorting through the faces of the news staff. How many of them had seen these awful pictures? She couldn't tell who might have witnessed her humiliation. Those who glanced up scarcely acknowledged her stare. Finally a pair of eyes met hers and engaged but the sports writer to whom they belonged merely looked thoughtful for a moment, obviously unaware of her chagrin or any hidden reason behind it, and turned away.

A couple of other people shot her curious looks as she stood paralyzed outside the darkroom, but nothing seemed to register as they returned to their phone conversations or set their attention back on their monitors or resumed browsing through afternoon issues of competing newspapers.

Who in this place could she trust? Did she dare trust anyone?

Marsh. She caught her breath, trying to gain control of the irrational fear spiraling through her. Where was he? She couldn't remember where he said he was going.

He'd given her a beeper number.

Frantically, she rummaged through her purse. No luck. She dumped the contents onto her desk before she snapped open her coin purse. There it was, the scrap torn out of her spiral notebook. She caught it up with both hands and pressed it to her mouth. Thank God.

She dialed the phone, then hung up to wait. But pondering her discovery, she couldn't bear to sit. To be still. To be idle. She needed to calm down. She eased into her desk chair and tried to slow her breathing and think of any other explanation for this outrage. But every avenue led straight back to Wesley. Maybe Marsh would have a plausible explanation. She wrung her hands. *Please let him call. Or, better still, come.*

What if Wesley returned to the office before Marsh arrived? Maybe she should put the pictures back where she found them.

"Like hell," she rasped, leaped to her feet and paced through the newsroom, made a U-turn at the exit and strode back.

As the paralyzing discovery and its accompanying horror began to ebb, a whole different emotion sluiced through her veins, sending rage to her extremities. Anna stared at the photo lab a moment before she paced slowly to her own desk and again eased into her chair. She slid her desk drawer open and placed the pictures and the negatives inside the small phone book, then pushed the drawer closed.

Her jaws ached from clenching and unclenching them and grinding her teeth. Exercising what she considered super human physical control, she relaxed her mouth.

Her good friend Wesley, so attentive, so thoughtful, so always there for her. How could he have thought up and carried out such a sickening, brazen scheme? She knew he was frustrated that she refused to consider him as a romantic figure, but he had to be emotionally twisted to come up with kidnapping her. The idea was like something out of a gothic tale.

She could think about it in brief little bits at a time, but it was so obvious. Wesley was the one person with the information necessary to have perpetrated it. He scheduled the interview and the pictures that put them at the scene at the right time. No one would consider it unusual to see either of them there. He had been shooting pictures around the university for years. Naturally, he would know about tunnels undercutting the entire campus, the ones Marsh had described. Wesley had probably taken pictures of the honeycomb sometime, maybe done an entire layout on them in years past.

As to what had provoked such extreme measures, she probably had a good idea about that too. "And they say Hell hath no fury like a *woman* scorned," she muttered.

She supposed he had not anticipated her reaction to the events. For one thing, he hadn't planned on her being in her menstrual period. Also, he had not anticipated her hormonal responses to his sexual stimulation. Nor could he have anticipated her crippling guilt over those responses.

No, as a psychologist, Wesley had turned out to be totally inept.

Then another, and a most upsetting possibility occurred to her. Had Marsh known? Had he been any part of it?

After several minutes of trying to wedge him into the scenario, she snorted. No. That was another of Wesley's bad oversights. No doubt, he expected summoning Marsh—his fast, womanizing friend—to propel her directly into Wesley's arms. Sure. He probably anticipated Marsh would be his usual flippant, aggressive self, come on with her and make Wesley appear the safer alternative. And that little ploy had almost worked, except that she and Marsh had established a relationship on solid ground quickly and beyond the limits any of them could have expected. And it was Marsh who had accomplished that, had won her trust with his completely unorthodox methods.

Strangely enough, friend Wesley was not as smart as he thought he was. He didn't know her as well as he thought, either, to summon the very person who could help her stumble and grope her way to a solution.

Also, Wesley underestimated Anna later, after the damage had been done. He didn't suspect she would have the fortitude to withstand another attack, this time a friendly one from the affable Marsh. Nor did he guess how Marsh's playful personality and strength of character would fortify her.

She fisted her hands, no longer feeling like a victim, but like a person wronged and gearing up to claim her pound of flesh from her tormentor. She worked her fingers, thinking how good it would feel to clamp those fingers around Stemmons' scrawny neck and squeeze the life right out of his miserable body. But she wouldn't take him on by herself. No, sir. He was a creep. A weasel. If she braced him alone, what might he do? A weasel cornered? He was Wesley the weasel. It was the perfect designation for such a loser.

She grit her teeth. She didn't need Marsh. If he came now, he might try to protect Wesley from her revenge. She felt her courage expanding, and her fury, too. She could take on either one or both of them at once. She could manage this match on her own. She didn't need Marsh or Ware or anyone else in her corner cheering. She was once again in charge of her own destiny, thank you very much. And she was beginning to hatch an idea about exactly what she should do.

Anna picked up the phone, dialed the police department and asked for Lieutenant Archer. She sounded more collected than she felt, so calm that the seething rage in her own voice frightened her.

Archer answered. "Hello, Ms. Fulenweider, what can I do for you?"

"Today, Lieutenant, it's what I can do for you. I have found our villain."

He swallowed loud enough for her to hear. "You have? Well, good for you. Who is it?"

"How long will it take you to get to the newspaper office?"

"Don't you want to tell me who you think this guy is?"

"No, I think it would be better for you to see the hard evidence I have before we begin speculating and arguing."

"Are you there at your office?"

"Yes."

"I'll be there in ten minutes. Sit tight."

As she sat, she fretted. What had possessed her good friend, her confidant, to do such a despicable deed? What had he expected to gain? Had he expected her to appreciate such reprehensible behavior?

She swung around in her chair, looking at her coworkers, her working world. Hers and Wesley's. She had always been glad when they were assigned to cover things together. He was the best darn photographer in town, maybe even the state. This was ludicrous. What was he, some kind of a control freak? Did he have some deep, emotional scar? What outcome had he expected? Or had he even thought it through to an ending?

No need stewing about it. She could let the police and Dr. Ware come up with reasonable explanations. Provide the details. She had done the hard part. She had uncovered the culprit. She smiled a little to herself. Don't mess with a capable, independent woman. Especially not when her hormones are seriously engaged.

Archer didn't wait for the elevator. He bounded up the stairs to the newsroom two-at-a-time, then stopped cold when he saw her sitting, rocking back and forth in her office chair, a peculiar smile on her pretty face. The only sign of turmoil was her impatient fingers tapping out a rhythm on the top of her desk.

"Come sit," she offered, after she saw him. She stood and rolled another chair around for him. She had placed the developed pictures of the beauty queens out on the desk and covered them with a single sheet of newsprint. The negatives of her were in the drawer.

When he was seated, Anna carefully lifted the paper.

The lieutenant allowed a low whistle. "Were these taken through the peepholes?"

"Yep."

"How'd he do it?"

"I don't know. But I recognize the angle."

He flashed her a sheepish smile, as if he were embarrassed for them to be viewing these pictures together.

"You said you know who did it."

"Yep."

"Okay, who?"

"Stemmons."

"Nooo." He squinted at her skeptically as he groaned the one word response, yet she had the impression he was not altogether shocked. She waited, however, studying him. "Why would he abduct you, Ms. Fulenweider? Did he think you had seen him taking these? That you might turn him in?"

"No, I don't believe so. I think he liked me and he wanted me to like him back."

"Just because he took these unauthorized pictures, of course, doesn't necessarily mean he's your kidnapper."

She really didn't want to drag out the pictures of her, if she didn't have to do it. "Okay, let's look at the situation. He's the one who set me up to be there. Normally, the society editor covers pageants. He knows my habits. Knows I always get to an interview early. The girls were on stage, rehearsing a group skit. Everyone was out front watching them rehearse. He counted on my being there, alone, snooping around like I do."

"Do you think he expected you to spot the peepholes and try to find out where they went?"

She nodded confirmation. "Yes. And then he grabbed me."

Archer gave her a jaundiced look. "Everything about what you've just said is speculation, of course. You're a good looking woman, Ms. Fulenweider, but...well, maybe you're letting your ego run a little wild here."

"I don't think so."

"Even if he thought you were the Queen of Sheba, I don't see what he hoped to gain. Did he plan to coerce you into...*liking him back*?"

She grimaced at hearing her own words played back at her. "No, he planned to stimulate me sexually, make me crazy with wanting a phantom, then somehow he'd let me know he was the guy."

"Is that what the perp did, then? He stimulated you...ah... sexually?"

She nodded, feeling the blush heat her face as her voice dropped. "Yes."

"But you didn't get to liking him at all, did you? His plan didn't work?"

She couldn't look at him. "Well, this is the part I had all the trouble with. You see, much to my mortification, it did work." She avoided his eyes as she continued. "I don't have a lot of sexual experience. What I mean is, I didn't realize how stimulating hard-core foreplay might be." She shot him a look, wishing she didn't have to spell all this out. "To put it bluntly, my sexual experience has been limited. I'm what you might call *sexually challenged*." She flashed an apologetic grin and shrugged.

Archer glowered as if he didn't believe her. Obviously he was as uncomfortable delving into this subject as she was, but a moment later professionalism took the lead to overcome his awkwardness.

"So, what went wrong? Why didn't he pursue this plan to its natural conclusion? Was it your behavior? Did you say or do something to change his mind?"

"No. I had just started my period."

Archer's mouth dropped. "And he couldn't...ah...he didn't want to...ah?"

"Right."

"Okay," the detective yielded, allowing her to win the point. "So why didn't you identify him as the perp?"

"I didn't know it was him. He wore masks and clown costumes and gloves. He whispered and there was the constant hum of motors. It was dark and shadowy."

"But he's skinny and you told the cop who found you..."

"That the guy was big and soft."

Archer puckered and looked at the floor as if he were deep in thought. Finally, he looked back at her. "You know he's going to deny it. How can you say for certain he's the man when you stated flatly you didn't know him and it turns out to be someone you work with every day; someone whose voice you should have recognized; whose movements and walk should have been at least familiar to you."

She didn't know if Archer was playing devil's advocate or if she was losing credibility. As much as she hated to do it, she opened the desk drawer, produced the telephone book and opened it to retrieve the negatives of her lying nude, shackled on the mattress.

Archer's expression darkened as he squinted at the first one, then the second, holding them up to the ceiling light. His chin jutted forward squaring his jaws like a bulldog as his eyes met hers. His question emerged as a hiss. "Where is the son of a bitch?"

"On assignment, according to the sign-out sheet. He's supposed to be back by four-thirty."

They both looked at the wall clock. Four o'clock, straight up.

"I want to see his darkroom."

"You don't need a search warrant?"

"Nah. It's an open work place. He has no expectation of privacy here. Your permission as an employee is good enough."

She led him into the photo lab and pointed out Stemmons' area. Archer rifled through the open drawer. He put a dozen pictures into an envelope, added a fistful of negatives and slipped the envelope into his coat pocket.

"What about the yeast smell?" he muttered as he sorted the pictures. "Do you have an explanation for that?"

"Yes. I was thinking about that while I was waiting for you. What better way to mask the smell of the chemicals he works around all day long, odors I might easily have recognized that to cover them with a stronger odor?"

"Has Stemmons ever asked you out? I mean on a regulation date?"

"Yes, when I first started working here. But that was more than a year ago."

"You didn't want a biracial relationship?"

"I didn't care what color he was. I don't date guys I work with. I learned a hard lesson about that once. This guy and I got pretty involved. When we split, things were complicated, more so because we had to see each other every day in the same office. It fouled everything—our friendship and our working relationship. People in the office felt obligated to choose sides, his or mine. Everyone was miserable."

"This was a real screwball idea, you know," Archer said, waving a hand over her bare desktop which indicated he was referring to the pictures and the negatives which were no longer there. "I can't imagine it would have worked. You're a bright young woman. Could it have?"

She shrugged. "It might have. I was not familiar with the raw sensations my captor aroused. I have never," she bit her lips, "petted real heavily."

Archer flushed, but plunged ahead, obviously uncomfortable. "What sensations?"

"Well, that's not something I really want to talk about right now, if you don't mind. All I can say is, it was a novel idea, I mean his baiting me that way."

"Are you saying it did work?"

"While I was isolated in the dark, yes, I think it probably did."

"Do you have any permanent...ah...problem...that way?"

She ducked her head to avoid looking at him. "I'm not sure."

Nodding, Archer shifted his gaze back and forth between the door and Anna.

"Has Marsh been able to help...straighten you out?"

She laughed. "The guy doesn't need a publicist, does he?"

Archer gave her a lofty grin. "Well, some fellows have a natural finesse with women. I think its chemistry. It's pretty obvious. If you don't happen to have it, you notice the ones who do."

"And you've pegged Marsh as one who does?"

He fought the grin and the freshening flush, but finally let it go and nodded. "Yeah, I'd say probably so. Didn't you?"

She sputtered a little laugh. "Yeah, I'd say probably he does have some natural gifts in that department."

They both were laughing as Marsh and Wesley strolled into the newsroom in lock step. Anna leaped to her feet and sobered. Her look prompted both of the new arrivals to turn angry stares on Archer.

He glowered back at them.

Marsh snapped first. "What are you doing here, Lieutenant?"

"What'd you say to her?" Wesley spat a split second later.

"It wasn't me, guys." He looked at Marsh. "Joe, your good friend Stemmons here is the man responsible for traumatizing our girl's psyche. He's the guy who snatched her."

Marsh leveled a hard stare at his boyhood friend.

Wesley gave Marsh a wry look, then stared back at Archer, obviously trying to make up his mind whether or not to brazen it out. But the detective remained stoically calm.

"The good news is: she's cured," Archer said. "Got well after one enlightening trip into Stemmons' darkroom this afternoon, all by herself, when no one else was around."

Wesley's eyes shot from the detective to Marsh to Anna and he sputtered as if unable to decide which road to take. His expression became wide-eyed disbelief, but the denial slowly deteriorated when he looked into Anna's defiant face.

They stared into each other's eyes a long moment before he attempted a wicked grin and broke the silence, his voice low. "You wanted me, Anna. Don't try to say you didn't. You wanted a black man. You wanted him bad. You..."

Her eyes fairly sparked beneath arched, defiant brows. "Well, I don't want him now, Stemmons. When I get to exercise my free will and make my own choices, I don't want his filthy hands or his perverted mind anywhere near me. That's the one most important thing you overlooked. You forgot to consider what *I* wanted."

"I know you, Anna. I'm your best friend. I know what you need and I want to give it to you. I understand you, baby, like no other man, black or white, ever can or will understand you."

She concentrated on putting just the right amount of disdain in her expression and inflection in her voice. "You are pathetic. Do you know that? The strongest feeling I have ever had for you, Stemmons, and I have it right now, in spades, pardon the pun, is pity."

His eyes rounded and his face twisted into a menacing glare, but before he could level a response, a familiar clatter silenced him.

The noise was Lieutenant Archer producing handcuffs. That detestable sound of metal on metal jolted Anna and she whirled, defiance etched into her face and in her posture. She felt an overwhelming sense of relief as Archer caught Wesley's shoulder and whipped him around, at the same time grabbing the man's right hand. He attached the cuffs, then tightened them until Anna saw the metal pinch into the flesh at Stemmons' wrists.

But Wesley wasn't through. "You're gonna keep on remembering me, Anna. Remembering how much you wanted me. Think of me when you're alone in your bed at night, when you're wishing someone was there touching you like you know I can touch you, 'cause I will damn sure be thinking of you, and remembering, and biding my time until..."

He choked and swallowed the next words as Archer shoved him rudely toward the exit and out, shooting a quick, apprehensive look back over his shoulder.

When Anna turned around to see what had prompted Archer's abrupt departure, she caught Marsh's expression and realized the reason for the detective's haste.

Joe's hands were balled into fists and his jaw was set. He stared at the departing pair and trembled with what appeared to be rage.

Chapter Twenty

Anna was there before the doorbell quit ringing. Joe Marsh smiled to himself as she rattled the security chain. No more anxious questions through the closed door. He would call that stupendous progress. His three weeks in town had been productive, if not what he would consider a complete success.

She wiped her hands on a dishtowel as she backed up to let him in. Most of her straw-colored hair was confined to a single braid, but rebellious tendrils looked entirely appropriate. Her clear skin had a sheen. There was no hint of make-up, no camouflage to veil the wholesome glow that was so her.

Obviously a little self-conscious, she diverted her eyes to avoid looking directly at him. God only knew what she might see if she looked too closely. Reading his thoughts at that moment might make her bolt and run right out of there, if she guessed at all the turmoil going on under his studiously calm exterior.

It was a wonder to him that she couldn't smell the raw emotions singed and exposed there where his heart used to be; a wonder that organ, pounding like a trip hammer, didn't frighten the bejeebers out of her.

"Lock up, will you?" She tossed the words over her shoulder as she hurried back to the kitchen.

Joe shut the door, flipped the dead bolt and replaced the chain.

Another sign of progress: she was willing to be locked inside with him. Alone. Yeah, this trip, using up all his vacation time, even betraying his oldest friend in the world had definitely been worthwhile.

He paced through the living room memorizing things— the news magazine lying on the floor by the sofa, open to an article on euthanasia; a "Family Circle" beside it, flipped open to a color picture and recipe for carrot cake, little indications of her range of interests.

His smile felt forced, bitter sweet. He didn't want to leave, but he had come to that inevitable fork in the road. He had to go, for her sake. Nah, he knew better than that. He had to leave for both their sakes. He'd kept a tight rein, but he could feel his control slipping. Touching her wasn't enough any more, had never been enough, really, not since that first day when every brush, every look, made her quail.

She glanced at him through the pass-through from the kitchen. "Sit."

Oh, yeah, he was her trained dog, all right, responding to single-word voice commands like any other whipped hound. Obediently, he sat on a chair-backed bar stool and looked at her. What had happened to him?

Seeing the irony of the situation, he flashed her a wry smile, one she didn't see as she grabbed a rubber spatula and stirred the contents of a large saucepan. Some kind of white creamy goo had her full attention. Heaven only knew what he would give to have her focus on him that way. Actually, he pretty well understood Wesley's hang-up about her. Was understanding it better every day.

She stirred frantically until she appeared to have the bubbling concoction under control.

"What?" She said it as if prompting him to continue an ongoing conversation. It was another of her habits which had become gut-wrenchingly familiar.

He watched as a wispy strand of hair swung into her face. Using the back of her wrist, she brushed it aside, still concentrating on the creamy substance which appeared to be getting thicker as she stirred. Suddenly she slid the pan off the burner and doused the power.

He hooked his heels into a rung on the barstool, giving him a lap, an effort to hide the effect being alone with her frequently had on him.

She tossed the hot pad on the countertop, again flipped away the errant strand and looked at him. "Okay, I'm all yours. What's up?"

All his? He wished. Then she would for sure discover what was up—what was always up and ready for action when she was in the room. They were seldom alone these days, however, since Wesley's arrest and arraignment, and Joe felt almost smug that she seemed so relaxed around him now.

"I'm leaving."

Her smile dimmed as she studied him. "Meaning?"

"I'm going home. To Colorado."

There was a long silence. He watched her reaction, aware of every nuance in her body language, facial expression, the way she cleared her throat twice, then again.

He'd expected her to be mildly surprised but her response shifted from thoughtful concern to what? If he didn't know better, he would think it was alarm.

Was that alarm? Her shoulders drooped as they did when she was fatigued. What was going on in that creative little brain of hers?

She looked away. "I didn't expect you to...ah...be leaving so soon."

He wanted to be mature, to help her handle what he had not expected to be an eventuality that was all that traumatic for her. Of course, he probably should have guessed there would be some residual reaction. She had become dependent on him, which was not a good thing, something Ware had warned him to avoid as far as possible.

"You're fine now. All well. Ware says the sessions are really showing your progress. You don't need me hanging around any more. You don't need your crutch. You're ready to go on your own."

When she remained silent, in an effort to fill the awkward quiet he began repeating himself. "You don't need me to lean on any more, or anyone else."

There he'd said everything he'd rehearsed, some of it twice. He should shut up and leave, but he waited, studying her reaction, hoping for a denial but, in reality, expecting blatant indifference.

Her eyes flashed. She started to speak, then bit her lips, bottling the words. She pulled the dishtowel from her shoulder where she'd draped it after answering the door and mopped her face. She seemed to be stalling. Without taking his eyes off her, he swiveled slowly back and forth in the bar stool, monitoring her every move, and waited.

When she finally looked at him, her eyes were wide and glistening. Tears? For him? Now there was a surprise.

Her words came in a whisper. "I don't want you to go."

"You knew I'd be leaving sooner or later."

"But you said you wouldn't leave until I was ready."

"You *are* ready. You might just not know it yet."

She stiffened. "And you *do* know...what's right for me? What I need? And, as usual, you will act accordingly."

"Well." He was uncertain about his footing on this surprising ground. Her reaction was unexpected. What was she trying to say? "You know the only reason I came here in the first place, Anna, was because Wesley thought I could help you find your way back to being yourself."

"And you think I'm there? Or now that Wesley's gone, you think all agreements are off? Or are you just tired of baby-sitting me?"

He barked a laugh at the irony of it. He *wanted* to baby-sit her—and that was only the tip of the iceberg. He'd like to keep on baby-sitting her every day. For a long time. For the foreseeable future. Maybe for the rest of their lives.

Whoa, now! That was another little shocker.

But she didn't need a caretaker hovering over her anymore and he was getting restless playing the part of her trusted lap dog, having her scratch behind his ears when it was convenient, and ignore him the rest of the time.

She took several reluctant steps toward him, then stuck out her hand. Her mouth quivered. "Good-bye, then. Thank you very much for coming. And good luck."

He had prepared himself for this moment.

She wished him luck. Great. Part of his pep talk to himself had centered on plenty of other fish in the sea, but he had been seining a long time without pulling up a keeper. Not until now. He had never known, had never even seen a woman like the one standing before him. The way she looked, the way she laughed, the way she argued. She was perfect for him.

Often distracted, a clutterer, nosy to the point of butting into the big middle of other people's lives uninvited, a woman who frequently forgot to comb her hair or put on fresh lipstick.

She might not be perfect by anyone else's standards, but she was perfect for him. He found her many little foibles and idiosyncrasies charming. Alluring. Damn sexy.

He had been totally seduced by her early on—by the insecurity she kept hidden behind her confident facade. He actually admired her disregard for appearances and the way she delved into people, mining to the parts she found valuable in each of them.

He liked the self-deprecating way she could turn a joke or a glib comment on herself.

Physically, he had never seen a more perfect specimen. Of course, he had always been a boob man and she had a set of what he considered the most exquisite breasts he had ever seen.

The damage done to her psyche by her ordeal had almost been countered, leaving her a wiser and, possibly, more compassionate person.

Again she poked her hand toward his gut, stepping closer. Yielding, he grinned and took the offered hand, intending only to shake it firmly, then release it. The handshake was businesslike, until she wrapped her long, cool fingers around his thumb, swaddling it, pressing her palm against his.

Anna clasped Joe's thumb in a death clutch, wrapping it with her other hand to reinforce her grip on him, and to warm herself by the body heat which always seemed to emanate from him.

As usual, it was as if he could read her mind and recognize her need. He remained seated on the bar stool and tugged her hand, signaling, pulling her closer. He parted his knees and she glided comfortably into that safe, intimate haven.

"You're going to manage just fine without me, Anna Banana-my-girl."

She grimaced. "Don't call me that."

"Okay." He bowed his head, his nose nearly touching her breasts, before he became aware of how close they were and straightened, flashing her a frown.

Obviously he was uncomfortable with their proximity. Well, that was just tough. She didn't want him to leave her, to again be several hundred miles away. She wanted him here, close enough to see him, to talk to him, to touch him when she needed reassuring. She wanted to tell him all that. But how could she when she wasn't sure how he felt about her—not about the psychological cripple she had been, but about the woman she was.

She couldn't.

So, what was she going to do? Cut him adrift? He wanted to go. He'd sacrificed his time, his expertise, his patience to get her functioning normally. Now he was through with all that. And she could understand.

He thought he was her crutch. He was so much more than that. He was her laughter and her calm. He was the reason she could turn out the lights at night before she slept. He had schooled her and taught her to throw the punches required to pound her way out of that bag of suffocating fear.

Tell him, she chided herself. He was leaving anyway. What did she have to lose, except a little pride? Pride—as if she had any left around him. She should say it out loud. He might as well know.

Finally, it was her own innate nosiness that convinced her. She wanted to see his reaction to her revelation. Maybe he would be horrified, repulsed, knowing her secrets the way he did.

Or maybe she would see pity in his face. That would be unbearable, but she could endure it long enough for him to hit the door and be gone.

But the very worst response of all would be if he looked determined, willing to sacrifice himself by pretending to care about her in a valiant effort to bolster her wimpy ego. That wouldn't do. She didn't intend to let him martyr himself.

She snorted, disgusted with her own cowardice. She hated all this speculation. *Don't think about it*, she chided herself again. *Go with your gut. That's what he'd tell you to do.*

His head was bowed so she could no longer see his face.

Steeling herself, Anna intentionally brushed her breast against his temple. He jerked his head back, turned slightly and gave her a questioning frown.

Surely he couldn't have thought the move was accidental. He knew her, knew how sensitive she was to physical contact.

There was just the hint of a smile on his lips as he tilted his face and lowered it to rub his cheek against the tantalizing breast.

Their hands, still clasped, snaked together in a sensuous dance. Anna closed her eyes, not wanting him to see how their mingling heat melted her inside.

Slowly, he placed his free hand on her waist, then let it drift, following the line from her waist down over her hip to her thigh, then back up. He opened his mouth and settled it on her near breast as he moved the roving hand to the small of her back and pressed her closer, more tightly between his legs.

Her breath caught and something low in her stomach tightened.

She made a conscious effort to exhale and noticed that his breathing, too, had grown ragged, coming and going with an audible rasp.

"Can you finish that later?" he asked, indicating the pan of pie filling.

"Yes." Her voice sounded unusually husky to her own ears. "Would you like to go sit on the sofa and neck a while?"

He raised his eyes to hers and laughed lightly. "If you want to, it'd be all right with me. You know me. I'm easy. Putty in your hands."

It was her turn to laugh lightly. "I know."

He stood without releasing her hand and guided her toward the sofa. She balked. "There's more room on the bed."

He looked at her suspiciously. "Do you have any idea what you're doing?"

She giggled as she stepped up to lead him toward the bedroom.

"Look, Joe, I can be like your manager or your trainer or something, but you're going to have to fight your own way out of this bag yourself—get over this hang-up you've got."

He yanked their linked hands, swung her around to face him and lowered his hungry mouth to hers, silencing not only her words, but her thoughts...her inhibitions...her fears, as she wrapped her arms around him and held on tightly, excited and mentally preparing herself for whatever pleasure might be coming next.

Printed in the United States
127570LV00003B/4/P

9 780937 660119